MARS

MIKE MARS FLIES THE DYNA-SOAR

Other Books in the Mike Mars Series:

MIKE MARS ASTRONAUT

MIKE MARS FLIES THE X-15

MIKE MARS AT CAPE CANAVERAL

MIKE MARS IN ORBIT

USAF

Mike Mars Flies the Dyna-Soar

DONALD A. WOLLHEIM

ILLUSTRATED BY ALBERT ORBAAN

DOUBLEDAY & COMPANY, INC.
GARDEN CITY, NEW YORK
1962

Library of Congress Catalog Card Number 62–11373

Printed in the United States of America
First Edition

CONTENTS

Special Acknowledgment Notice

The author wishes to extend his personal thanks for the assistance rendered in the preparation of this book by the United States Air Force. In particular, thanks are due to Major James F. Sunderman, Chief of the USAF Book Program, and to the ISO staff of Holloman Air Force Base, headed by Lieutenant Colonel Charles Harris and including Mr. George F. Meeter. Acknowledgment is also given to the Information Offices of Davis-Monthan AFB, Randolph AFB, The Martin Company, and Boeing Airplane Company. In making these acknowledgments, the author wishes to make clear that he has not had access in any fashion to any classified material and that his portrayal of the Dyna-Soar and operations connected with it is purely speculative.

MIKE MARS FLIES THE DYNA-SOAR

CHAPTER ONE

HURRICANE HILDA

If you had just come into the room and did not know where you were, you would have supposed that it was a very dull place to be. It was a large chamber and there were no windows. The walls were gray-painted, undecorated, and the main fixtures were panels with black plastic fronts studded with dials, little lights, and buttons marked with numbers. There were a number of gray-painted metallic swivel chairs, very businesslike, set in the floor before several of these panels. Sitting in them were men patiently and silently watching the instruments.

But if you stayed in the room, you would quickly get the feeling that something very exciting was going on. The concentration of the men, the little group of people standing in a cluster behind one of the men, looking over his shoulder at the roll of tape slowly unwinding under glass in the machine before him, revealed their tension. Still you would have to stand with them, study what was going on, and then, maybe with a few questions, you would know something that very few Americans were privileged to know.

"His respiration is steady," said the man reading the tape. "Canton Island reports no change."

One of the standing group, a big elderly man sporting a little black beard and mustache, nodded. His sharp blue eyes read the coded message on the tape over the operator's shoulder. "Yes, very good. He sleeps well."

"Heartbeat is sound and strong," said another of the standing group, who had walked softly over to glance at the readings on another instrument. "Comes in on the sleeping pattern, just like the last time around." The speaker was a young man, bronzed from the sun, his freckled face youthful enough to make one wonder at the lieutenant's bars that were clipped to the collars of his short-sleeved Air Force khaki shirt. In shorts, he looked like a high school athlete.

"At sleeping, your friend Johnny Bluehawk is real good. *Ja*," said the third of the four standing watchers. This was the stocky gray-haired doctor of space medicine, Hugo Holderlin. "We not have trouble with him like with your readings. With you— Ha, nothing we get!"

The sandy-haired pilot laughed. "Well now, Doc, that wasn't my fault. Come around some night at Skyhook and see how well I can snooze!"

"And it wasn't fair of you to mention it," said the fourth party in a soft but angry whisper. The speaker was a pretty girl somewhere in her teens.

"Vivian is right," said the bearded man, who was

the world-famous pioneer aviation scientist, Dr. Merlin Van Ness, and who had given his pony-tailed daughter permission to join them in this special chamber.

One of the men spoke softly. "Hawaii reporting contact now," he said. "No change in the readings. Everything very smooth."

The four watchers were silent, watching the new records come in. For what was being recorded on the instruments were the second-by-second reports from an object in space, a capsule in orbit around the world. Fifteen times this new artificial moon of Mother Earth had gone around the parent planet, and in it a man lived and breathed, had eaten, had talked and joked with this room down on the surface of the world below, and was now deep in sleep. Asleep in space—even as he slept the wires and sensitive electrodes attached to his body silently sent down their messages.

This was the telemetry room of the National Aeronautics and Space Administration building at Cape Canaveral, or rather at Patrick Air Force Base fifteen miles away from the launching pads of the Atlantic Missile Range. The man in orbit was one of the six remaining astronauts of America's top secret space project, the Quicksilver program.

Mike Mars, the young Air Force lieutenant, didn't mind the joshing that Dr. Holderlin had given him, even if Vivian Van Ness was determined to take it the wrong way. Mike had experienced the German scientist's humor before, and he knew it was meant well. Besides, his own first flight in orbit had indeed failed to return a full report.

There had been a little trouble from an explosive planted in the capsule by a renegade member of their own group. Fortunately, Mike had been able to patch it up and everything came out all right. But they never did get anything like a completely satisfactory record of his physical reactions and the inner workings of the capsule from his flight.

Now this present orbital flight of Mike's best friend and fellow astronaut, Johnny Bluehawk, was a real dandy. They had launched Johnny almost twenty hours ago, and he was still making the regular transit of the Earth.

It had followed by about a month Mike's own flight. Project Quicksilver was a crash program. They had sacrificed a good deal of the cautious experimentation that publicly acknowledged space experiments carried on; they were deliberately taking risks more experienced and older astronauts were forbidden to make. But they were all volunteers for it, and they knew what they were getting into.

Now, Johnny's flight was to last a day, and the day in space was almost over. His telemetry readings, kept in continuous sequence by relays from NASA stations located all around the world, would give invaluable information. There were four other members of Mike Mars' team, and they were scattered around the world at various other stations, observing and

sometimes engaging in conversation with Johnny up in the sky as he passed overhead.

"Reading is changing," said one of the NASA operators suddenly. They all went over, looked.

"He's waking up," said Holderlin. "See how his heartbeat picks up as he regains consciousness."

"Watch the respiration. He's breathing deeper, and the change in the atmosphere of the capsule is immediately noticeable," said Merlin Van Ness.

"It's wonderful," whispered Vivian to Mike. "We

studied in school how the body slows down during sleep and then regains normal energy when awake, and it's wonderful how we can see it happening here."

Mike nodded. "Even more so when we know these readings are coming from somewhere a hundred miles above the Pacific Ocean in outer space where it's black and airless and the stars are always shining."

The black-bearded scientist held up a hand. There was a voice coming in, at first faint, then stronger as the relaying stations picked it up, passed it along to Florida.

"Hello, Vandenberg," said the voice, and Mike recognized the strong clear tones of his fellow astronaut, the Cheyenne jet pilot of the U. S. Air Force. "I can see the California coast coming up now. Do you read me?"

They could not hear the reply from Vandenberg Air Force Base on the Pacific Coast, but in a little while they heard Johnny's voice calmly reading off the dials inside the capsule, checking them against their telemetry readings.

Van Ness nodded. "Excellent. One more orbit, and then we'll prepare to bring him down. Shall we go down for a bite to eat first, while we have still an hour or so left?"

The other three nodded. Johnny was in good hands; they didn't need to be present, and they hadn't slept too well themselves during the long vigil.

The four went out, rode down in the elevator to

the cafeteria in the building. They gathered around a little table, talked a while.

Mike Mars was always a bit uneasy in the presence of Dr. Van Ness' daughter. She was so—hero-worshiping was his thought—and he wasn't too anxious to get mixed up with her. He was interested in space flight and in aviation. His work on Project Quicksilver was all-important to him. There'd be plenty of time for girls when the important work was done.

But Vivian, as the daughter of their project's director, was a privileged character. She made a nuisance of herself, though she wasn't aware of it, for her interest in aviation and astronautics was quite real. She was shooed away now, after they had had a bite. Dr. Van Ness pointed out that she was due back at school, that she had been with them long enough. She wanted to stay and watch the recording of the landing, but her time had run out.

So Vivian reluctantly bid the three men good-by and left. The three sighed in slight relief after she'd gone.

They returned upstairs leisurely. When they reentered the telemetry room, they sensed a certain change.

"What's up?" asked Van Ness of the man in charge.

The man looked up from his meters. "Nothing, Doctor," he said. "Everything is exactly as expected. Quicksilver Two is now crossing Africa on its last lap around. However . . ."

". . . now officially designated Hurricane Hilda."

"However what?" asked Mike quickly.

The man tapped a message spiked on his board. Mike picked it up, and he and the two others looked at it.

"There's been a sudden change in the weather readings in the Caribbean," said Mike, interpreting the routine report from the weather office.

"Yes," said Van Ness slowly. "In the area where Johnny Bluehawk will be coming down, there has been a steady change for several hours. I had hoped nothing would come of it, but this looks bad."

"It looks to me, sir," said Mike, recalling his long hours of study on weather and meteorology which had been part of the training program for the astronauts, "like the makings of a hurricane."

"Makings . . ." said Merlin Van Ness. "More than that. Three hours ago I was informed that a tropical storm was brewing near that area. Now it has definitely developed and is moving in."

"Tropical Storm Hilda," said Mike Mars, reading a second message which had been tacked to the bottom of the first weather reading, "is now officially designated Hurricane Hilda."

"And Johnny's capsule is due to come out of orbit and come down to Earth right there!" said Dr. Van Ness.

CHAPTER TWO

IN THE EYE OF THE STORM

JUST how disturbing this news was, Mike Mars could appreciate. He had been the first of the Quicksilver astronauts to orbit the earth in a capsule and he knew just how risky it was—coming down out of orbit, passing through the first layers of the outer atmosphere, then passing through thicker and thicker air to the point where the little shell's retro-rockets would slow it down and finally the big parachute would open.

The parachute stage was the danger here. If instead of the calm Caribbean sea, the incoming space vehicle was to be confronted with a raging area of wild winds and furious gusts, it might mean total disaster. The parachute could be torn to bits; the capsule, which was without any capacity for gliding, would plummet wildly into the water, if it didn't first swing insanely in the winds.

"But what can we do?" he asked Dr. Van Ness, who was standing now before a wall chart in the telemetry room. The chart was a flat Mercator's projection map of the earth on which each turn of Johnny Bluehawk's capsule had been plotted.

"There are possibilities," said Van Ness. "One involves having him delay his re-entry pattern so as to come down not in the designated area near Puerto Rico but further out in the ocean beyond the margin of the storm. This is bad because we have no facilities there to rescue him—and though the storm will then be several hundred miles away, the water will probably be choppy from its effects.

"The other possibility is to have him continue on course, landing in the heart of the hurricane—which is its eye—and this area is always calm if you remember your meteorology studies."

Mike pondered that. "That's a big risk. Like bull's-eye targeting. Can he do it?"

Van Ness frowned, traced a line across the map. "I think he could maneuver himself if he had exact advice from the spot from second to second. Unfortunately, we have no planes in the area capable of coping with the hurricane. The destroyer *Bayard* is on the scene, though I wonder how they are making out. There are helicopters waiting at Ramey Field on the island, but they cannot contest the hurricane."

Mike grabbed his arm. "Listen. If there's a good fast jet ready here at Patrick, I can take it out there and keep above the winds. I could 'talk' him down. Why not let me try?"

Van Ness nodded. Instead of answering, he drew Mike out of the quiet telemetry room and went quickly to a telephone in the empty office near it. He made a call to the operations officer at the field. What

he heard evidently satisfied him. He nodded to Mike. "They've got one they can tune up at once. Now to find out from Colonel Drummond what's doing."

He got back on the phone, began making connections. Colonel Drummond, Van Ness, and Holderlin were the three directors of Space Task Group Q, and Drummond was on duty at the point of re-entry aboard the *Bayard*, along with Joe Stacey, one of Mike's comrades.

"Drummond there? Hello, Otis, how does it look out there? Bad, eh? Now listen to this . . ."

Finally, Van Ness hung up. "Drummond says the destroyer is heaving and pitching to beat all. The storm's all around them, and their visibility is almost nothing. He suggests Johnny take another turn around, maybe a few more until the storm moves on."

Mike shook his head. "Has he enough food and oxygen for that?"

The scientist replied that he did but that he didn't favor risking it. "We don't know what state of mind Johnny is in, and I don't want this thing kept on indefinitely."

He turned to Mike. "We're going to chance it. Johnny's got to come down this next time around—otherwise it will be three more orbits before he'll be over the right area again. We have about an hour to get out there. Can you do it?"

"Sure thing, Doctor," said Mike. "Let's go."

The two hastily left the NASA building, grabbed their waiting car, and sped over to the runways at Patrick. Mike hastily transferred to his pressure suit and jet flying equipment. Then, with only seven minutes lost, he climbed the short ladder into the cockpit of the waiting F-100, the supersonic jet interceptor that Patrick happened to have on hand.

Within another minute he was airbound and heading out across the ocean, away from Cape Canaveral, in a line toward an oceanic spot near Puerto Rico, several hundred miles away.

He took the jet up to its limit; he stretched out its speed and tore on. Somewhere up above the atmosphere, out where only moons and meteors belong, his best friend was racing around the world to meet him. One had half a planet to cross and was traveling at 18,000 miles an hour. The other had but a short distance—planetary standards—to cross, and was buffeting the air twelve miles up at 800 miles an hour. They would arrive at the same spot at almost the same time. Mike had to get there just soon enough to make it possible for Johnny to survive.

But in Mike's mind as he sat, with oxygen mask feeding him and pressure suit holding him snug and warm against the terrible sub-zero of the heights, was the question of whether or not he could do what would be required.

Over his earphones, he heard now and then Van Ness reporting on the situation. "Bluehawk is speaking with Hart Williams at the Australia station now. All is well. He has been informed of the problem."

Or, "Drummond reports hurricane still intense in vicinity of the destroyer. No possibility of helping Bluehawk until they can get out of the winds."

And later, "Bluehawk approaching Canton Island station. After his next point of crossing, at Hawaii, he will have to start coming down."

Below Mike the miles of ocean passed, with here and there the islands of the sea. Cuba was far down on his horizon and the Island of Hispaniola, Haiti, and the Dominican Republic were visible. Beyond he could see faintly an area of increasing darkness and clouds.

That would be Hurricane Hilda. Now, with the jet at full out, he came above it. Below him he could see the great boiling churning area of black clouds and stringing-out winds of rain and dust. The area covered by the mighty storm must have included hundreds of square miles. It covered a great

USAF

section of the sea below, and what it did not cover was disturbed and thunderous with waves and lone dangerous gusts of wind.

Somewhere below him in the storm was the sleek U. S. Navy destroyer with Drummond and the men who were waiting to pick up Johnny Bluehawk. Mike called them, and amid the stuttering of static from the lightnings that played below him he could hear the answering voice of the ship.

Where Mike was the sky was peaceful, but this quiet would do no good when the capsule came down lower. He circled the area and saw what he was looking for. The hurricane's winds, marked clearly by great sweeping streamers of black cloud, were circular, and he found that they seemed to be framing a section of ocean, a few square miles in width, that was calm, clear, and blue.

It would be the heart of the hurricane, the dead center. Outlined like the center of the target, this was the place. He spoke to the *Bayard*, giving the destroyer the exact location of the calm in the heart of the storm. He heard the destroyer acknowledge, announce it would try to buck the storm, batter its way through the encircling winds to reach this spot.

"Bluehawk has started his retro-rockets," came the voice of Van Ness from Cape Canaveral. "He's beginning his long sweep down, across America."

Mike glanced at his fuel gauges. With the additional wing tanks, he should be able to keep his position for another twenty minutes. Well, that ought to do it.

On and on he went, circling the hurricane in wide fast sweeps, while the progress of the capsule was announced to him moment by moment. There was a clicking sound and a relay was set up, and in a moment, he heard a familiar voice.

"Mike, I hear you're keeping a candle in the window for me," said Johnny Bluehawk's voice, apparently cheery and untroubled. "How's it look?"

Mike switched his sender on. "Keeping calm here. How's my wandering boy tonight?"

"Close in over Florida now, Mike," said the voice of his Cheyenne friend. "Coming out, and beginning to heat up. Rockets are on the beam, though. Everything is just as the doctor ordered."

"Everything but the reception committee, chief," said Mike. "It's a real ring-a-ding blow down here. And there's the *Bayard* now, coming into the clear."

Sure enough, he could spot a tiny dot entering the clear blue area outlined in the center of the hurricane.

Now Mike began to give Johnny exact instructions. "Keep on dropping. When I say hold, hold; when I say release your first chute, then do it, and don't delay."

"I've got you loud and clear," said Johnny, and his voice wasn't in the least shaky. "I'm lower now, and I can see a faint spot of gray on the ocean. That's the hurricane, I guess."

"O.K., chief," Mike answered. He turned his head

in the narrow confines of the cockpit, looked through the transparent hood. He searched the sky as the fast jet continued its wide swing. Then he saw a tiny dot, high up, coming larger even as he spotted it.

"You're in sight!" he called. Quickly he estimated the location of the dot, which showed flashes of red now and then as the tiny retro-rockets fought to slow its fall.

"Get set," he called. "One, two, hold . . . hold . . . three. Now!"

There was a faint puff from the swelling glistening dot high above. Then first a touch of white and in a few seconds a billowing of orange as the main chute opened.

Mike swung his fast Sabrejet around, tried to keep his eye on the falling capsule and on the clear heart of the hurricane below.

"Steady on," he said. "I think we've got it right."

The capsule came down, visible now, a tiny bottle shaped like a boy's top, glistening in red paint, now dirty somehow—which would be where the burning heat of re-entry had scorched the painted surface—swinging tightly in the thin air beneath a huge orange-and-white striped parachute.

It passed Mike's speedy plane, went on down, the metal space cabin helpless beneath it, down toward the great fury of the mighty hurricane.

Mike held his breath, swooped along near it, as near as he dared. Would it make dead center?

Like a slow-falling bomb, he watched it target. And then, in his ears on the radio beam from the *Bayard*, came a shout. "We see him! We see him! He's in the clear!"

CHAPTER THREE

SURPRISE PACKAGES

MIKE did not see the actual rescue because his fuel was running perilously low and because it would be highly dangerous for him to try to circle around too low in the storm area. But Johnny Bluehawk was rescued without a hitch. Of course, the original plans had called for a helicopter, hovering over his capsule as it floated in the water, to drop him a line as soon as the hatch blew open and Johnny could climb out.

No helicopter was available, but when the hatch had been thrown open by the little explosive charge placed there for that purpose, and Johnny Bluehawk, still in his pressurized suit, had climbed out, all went like clockwork. The inflatable life raft was tossed out, filled itself, and Johnny plunked himself into it.

While this was going on, the destroyer was closing in, its motor launch already coming down into the water. As the gray naval vessel came to a stop, the launch was released and sped on its way. In a few minutes, its crew had scooped the astronaut up and were racing back to the destroyer.

Hands on deck hauled Johnny up, and there was a quick outburst of cheers from the men on duty. But time was pressing. Colonel Drummond and the slender Joe Stacey, Navy aviator and fellow member of the Quicksilver program, were the first to reach Johnny on the deck. Following right behind was the destroyer's commander.

"Shall we try to save the capsule, Colonel?" this officer asked. "The hurricane is closing in, and I wouldn't want to chance being caught by the winds with our towlines out."

Drummond turned around quickly, scanned the threatening horizon. "Let's not risk it," he said. "Let's get things stowed away and get out of here."

The ship's captain seemed distinctly relieved. He turned, called out orders. As they scudded into the safety of the wardroom, Johnny looked back once more at the capsule; already the rough seas were capsizing it. In a few minutes it would sink completely.

The headquarters of Space Task Group Q was at the closely guarded private estate of Dr. Van Ness, a large secluded area in central Florida not too far from Orlando. Because the entire operation was to be kept under wraps, it was found best to house and train the young men there, rather than in the more public areas of such bases as Langley in Virginia or Brooks in San Antonio. In this way they could avoid the unwelcome attention of reporters and the publicity of the curious.

Johnny Bluehawk did not return to Skyhook, which was the name of the estate, for over two days. During this time he was undergoing very extensive examination to determine the effects of his prolonged period of zero gravity upon his system. Thus it was not until Saturday afternoon that Mike and Dr. Van Ness picked him up at the Air Force hospital and drove back through the semitropical roadside to their base.

Johnny seemed in very good spirits and Mike was relieved at that. "You don't seem any the more subdued for being alone all the time," Mike remarked.

"Ha!" Johnny laughed. "Wait till you get a long run like that. Actually I feel all right now, and I think everything is O.K. Isn't that what the checkups showed, Doc?" he asked Van Ness.

The bearded scientist, who was in the front seat of the blue official car next to the airman driver, turned his head and looked back at the two young men. "You're perfectly all right," he said. "But they're worried about your report of being sort of seasick a while."

"I think we can overcome that, sir," said Johnny seriously. "If we anticipate it, it'll be possible to throw it off."

"How's that?" asked Mike. "I didn't get any sick sensation myself."

The Cheyenne looked at him. "You weren't up long enough. Apparently it takes about three or four hours to begin to make a man sort of queasy in continued weightlessness. I felt odd then. Nothing too bad, but I think I know now what people mean by seasickness. A little will power could keep it in check."

"How'd you manage sleeping?" asked Mike.

"That—oh, that was all right. In fact that's a cure of sorts, because, when I woke up, the slight sensation of nausea was gone. I guess the body takes a while to adjust to a sensation of continuous falling."

Back at Skyhook the two were greeted by Joe Stacey and the other astronaut on hand, lanky Jack Lannigan, a six-foot redhead who shared with Joe the honor of being naval aviators in their group. The small group of technicians and helpers on hand cheered as Johnny got out of the car. He waved a hand to them.

"Wait till the next fellow goes up," he called. "A week will be something to cheer about!"

Mike grinned as they went on into the white-columned, old-fashioned main building which was their quarters and main offices.

Colonel Drummond was present there, poring over some papers. "We've got some studying to do of Johnny's charts," he called. "I want a brief conference after dinner tonight."

"Wash up, boys, I'm famished," called Jack. "We figured they'd never let this wild redskin out of the hospital. He's so weak!"

Johnny made a dash for Jack and the two scuffled a moment in fun. Then they went on and washed.

When Mike and Johnny came down and went into the big dining room, they were surprised to see that all the others were there before them looking very sober. Dr. Holderlin had arrived, and Van Ness and his wife and even the vivacious Vivian had turned up, school being out for the week end. As the two friends came in, they started to smile, but noticed the strange air of severity that was on every face.

"Hey," said Mike. "What's the matter? Why the sobersides?"

Colonel Drummond frowned. "Sit down, Lieutenants Samson and Bluehawk, we have some very serious business to take up with you two." He drew his eyebrows down in a scowl.

Now Mike Mars' real name wasn't actually Mars. He had been christened Michael Alfred Robert Samson, and when he had started going to school he used to put his initials on his books and his bike and things. They spelled out M.A.R.S. and in consequence his friends began to call him Mike Mars.

Mike didn't mind the name; in fact, he rather liked it because he had made up his mind to be a space flier while he was still in junior high. He had read up on astronomy and aviation and rocketry and had determined his ambition then and there. It was an ambition he had never lost track of and had carefully planned to follow.

It was this dream, the dream of someday going to the planet Mars itself, that had carried him through high school with high honors in his studies, that had established for him a firm code of honor which did not permit him to slacken on his work, which insisted on the completion of every assignment accurately and promptly. He had kept himself in shape and had been a good athlete.

This ambition had taken him eventually into the U. S. Air Force, where he had gone all the way up through the various training courses, had earned his wings as a prop plane pilot, then as a jet pilot, and finally as a supersonic fighter plane pilot.

It had been then that he had volunteered for the new Quicksilver project and had gone through the many tests that had eliminated all but seven men. His friend, Johnny Bluehawk, had been a jet pilot with him, and the two of them had stuck together through everything.

As a Project Quicksilver astronaut he had flown the experimental rocket plane, the X-15, into the space beyond the atmosphere. He had ridden a Redstone in another short visit to the void he dreamed of conquering, and finally he had made the first Quicksilver orbital flight in a space capsule.

But what had he done now that was wrong? Why was everyone so silent and so serious? Had something been bungled?

He sat down in his seat, filled with wonder. Johnny Bluehawk drew up his chair next to Mike and let his lips tighten. For a moment he wondered—had the space medicine doctors found something in his physical records during the flight—something that was going to disqualify him for future flights? But, then, what about Mike?

The two sat straight in their chairs. Colonel Drummond scowled at them again. He took an official-looking envelope from his pocket, withdrew a letter, and scanned it briefly. He looked up again at the two wondering youngsters.

"Samson and Bluehawk," he said. "I have an order here that concerns you two men. It is from Air Force headquarters in the Pentagon." He paused, cleared his throat.

What have we done? Mike thought desperately.

"According to this command, it is my duty now to ask you to remove the lieutenants' bars you are wearing on your shirts. Do so!"

Mike and Johnny automatically put their hands up, began to unscrew the single silver bar that each wore on his shirt collar. Around them the table was dead silent, all eyes staring hard at them.

Colonel Drummond reached into his pocket, drew out two small boxes. "Put these on instead, *Captains* Samson and Bluehawk," he announced, and stood up, reached over, and handed them the two packets.

Mike confusedly opened the little box while his Cheyenne friend was doing the same. Inside was a new insignia, two silver bars joined together.

Around the table there was a burst of applause and a cheer. In a second everyone was up and pounding the two young fellows on the back.

Then suddenly Mike and Johnny simultaneously gave vent to their feelings. "Yowee!" they shouted, and everybody laughed and shouted with them.

Captains Samson and Bluehawk

CHAPTER FOUR

DIVIDED WE CONQUER

SPACE TASK GROUP Q was a top secret operation, but even so, it was directed by the all-over space program set up in Washington. Each new step of its crash effort to be the first in space had to be discussed in the nation's capital. Thus it was not until a week later that two of the three directors, Van Ness and Holderlin, returned from the main offices of NASA to lay out the future program.

This delay did not mean that the astronauts present at Skyhook loafed the week away. Though Mike and Johnny had received promotions, this did not otherwise relieve them of the responsibility for continuing their studies. For study was always the main necessity for astronauts and those connected with the field.

"Do you think we're going to get a chance to ride the Saturn soon?" Mike asked Colonel Drummond one day that week.

The colonel shook his head. "Hard to say. I think there may be a couple things for you to do before that. For one thing, I am sure the study of Johnny Bluehawk's long orbital flight will make it necessary to try some variations on it. They are evaluating the tape records of it now."

"Gee, the Saturn booster is going to make a big difference," Johnny put in. "I can't see why we can't get a crack at the moon pretty soon now with it."

Mike nodded, but turned to his friend. "I think so, too, but you know how it is. We can't risk it until at least a reasonable chance is made. First they plan a two-man space cabin in orbit, and that will be before the moon shot."

The gray-haired Air Force colonel, a veteran of the air, turned his sharp, weather-wrinkled eyes on them. "You'll get the chance soon enough. You fellows know what you're up against. You volunteered to risk your lives on not-entirely-proven vehicles. You're expendable. Don't be in such a hurry to get spent."

"Ah," said Mike, "I know that, but I think we've got to make speed. Our country's future depends on it."

All four astronauts present, for Joe Stacey and Jack Lannigan were in the room, nodded. They were in agreement on that. None of them was there for fame and glory or fortune. They were young and ready. That's all they asked.

But they were impatient to know what was next, and so it was on a Sunday—not usually a workday—that the next program session was held, on the return of the other two directors with new plans.

The four astronauts sat around the long table in

their main study room; their three directors sat down with them, while one, Dr. Van Ness, plopped his leather case on the table and carefully unlocked it.

"Orin McMahan and Hart Williams," he began, while taking documents from his case, "are still touring the telemetry stations along the Australia and Pacific routes. They will be kept there, pending the next orbital flight."

"They get left out of things," said Mike quietly.

Drummond glanced at him. "Don't worry about them. They'll have plenty to do in the next couple years. Right now we need them where they are."

Van Ness finished pulling the papers out, then cleared his throat. "Gentlemen," he began, "we have two sets of assignments on hand for the immediate future. I will deal now with the first which arises directly from Bluehawk's recent orbiting."

He paused, and every eye was on him. "As you know," he went on, "Captain Bluehawk reported a period of slight nausea and what we call disorientation during much of his flight. This sensation, quite the same as what is called seasickness or airsickness, apparently made itself noticeable after he had been in space some seven hours.

"No such feeling was reported by others who have been in the state of weightlessness caused by orbital flight or sub-orbital flight a shorter time. Yet you men represent the finalists of a series of hard tests designed to weed out any who were prone to such motion sickness. We must assume from this that the human body, kept in a state of zero gravity or free fall, has a harder time to adjust to this the longer the state remains.

"Now this is serious where space flight is concerned. We cannot have space fliers ill, dizzy, confused, and nauseous and hope that they can perform any valuable work. If this sort of thing is going to prove permanent in all human beings after a few hours of space flight, then we will have to put back all our thinking for many more years. So this must be overcome."

There was silence around the table. The men looked somewhat worried. It was a serious thing.

"Accordingly, we are going to schedule a new orbital flight, which is going to last either one day or three days, depending on whether the experiments work out. During this long flight, the astronaut will attempt to overcome his feeling of motion sickness by the use of various techniques. We will study the results of these efforts and by them learn how to overcome this big hurdle.

"The next man scheduled to ride the capsule into orbit is Joseph Stacey. Are you willing to undergo this difficult tour?" The question was directed at the slender figure of the naval aviator, who was the shortest and lightest of the Q program astronauts.

"Sure am," said Joe quickly. "Ready and willing. I was hoping I'd get the chance."

"Good," said the bearded astronautics expert, "and you've got it. We are ordering an Atlas prepared and a capsule readied, and we hope to set a launch date in three weeks' time.

"During this time you will undergo another careful physical checkup and we will test your reactions to certain chemicals and drugs. We believe that by the use of such well-known remedies as dramamine and similar drugs, used every day with great success by airline passengers and seagoing tourists, we can overcome these sensations.

"We also intend to experiment at various times during your orbiting with alterations in the air of the capsule, with longer periods of sleep than that in which Captain Bluehawk indulged and which seemed effective with him."

"I'm sure we can lick this thing," said Dr. Holderlin at that point. "If worse comes to worst and we cannot, then we will have to wait for a bigger booster to put up a doughnut-shaped space cabin which will rotate on its axis. In that way we make artificial gravity and give the space flier something to rest his aching head on."

"I think it won't be so bad," said Johnny Bluehawk then. "Sure, I felt sort of sickish, but it didn't interfere with my observations and I kind of think I could get over it."

"Maybe, maybe, but we have got to be sure," said the space medicine expert.

Dr. Van Ness nodded. "That's one of the two things for us to do. This work can be done by Lannigan and Stacey, who will operate as a team on this next flight. We have still a different assignment here for Mike Mars and Johnny Bluehawk.

"It seems that another NASA program is reaching a testing phase. This is the development of the space glider part of the Dyna-Soar program. They are beginning to test this now and they need a man who has worked on the X-15 to check out this new space plane."

Mike and Johnny felt an electric thrill run down their spines. Dyna-Soar! They had heard a little about it but they had supposed it was not yet due. They leaned forward.

"Our two captains are going to get a chance to try out their new bars at a very old testing ground. You have heard of the White Sands Testing Grounds?"

Dr. Van Ness looked at the two young fellows and saw them glance swiftly at each other.

"Sure, Doctor," said Mike excitedly. "That's where our country's first rocket tests were made, way back in 1946!"

Dr. Van Ness nodded. "I was there then, myself, and I can tell you it was exciting. Now you're going out there, or more properly to the Air Force Missile Development Center at Holloman Air Force Base right next to it. They've got work for you to do—and I wish I had the time to go along. If I could be in two places at once, I'd do it."

Dyna-Soar and booster

"Well, sir," said Mike, smiling, "we'll drop you a line now and then—by missile mail!"

"Not on my head, you don't," chuckled the bearded scientist.

CHAPTER FIVE

WELCOME TO WHITE SANDS

Mike and Johnny left Skyhook early the next morning. They made their connections at Orlando and, carrying their traveling kits, managed to get a plane as far as Randolph Field in Texas where they spent the night. Next morning a plane picked them up and took them the rest of the way to Holloman.

The plane grounded gently at Holloman, and they stepped out to blink in the sudden glare of hot sun, clear blue sky, and wide flat barren desert. As they looked around, a lean bronzed man, sporting a slight mustache and wearing Air Force khakis, came up to them.

"Samson and Bluehawk?" he asked, and at their nods, "I'm Major Padgett. I've made the arrangements for you. I'm with the Space Development Group here, and you'll be working with me and my boys. Glad to have you aboard."

They shook hands as the major walked them toward the car that was awaiting. "We'd thought about putting you up at the base, but Colonel Drummond called me and thought it might be better if you fellows boarded with me at my place in Alama-

U.S. AIR FORCE

gordo. It'll be more comfortable, and besides he thought it would keep you out of circulation around here."

"Gee, that would be nice of you," said Mike. "You must be married, and maybe we can get some home-cooked meals."

"Sure thing, fellers," said the major. "Married, with two kids. So keep your lip buttoned up at home."

They climbed into the car and soon were speeding out of the base on toward the rocket town.

The sun was beginning to set and the effect on the approaching mountains was breath-taking. They sat silently and looked while the major told them something about the locality.

"Alamagordo grew up in the rocket age," he said. "It used to be a small town, a sort of western whistle stop, until they brought the captured German V-2 rockets out here to test them. Gradually a big rocket research industry grew up out here as the White Sands Proving Grounds became America's first space operations area. Now Alamagordo is a thriving little city and proud of it."

"This was Wild West country," put in Johnny Bluehawk quietly. "It was Apache territory and has quite a history."

"Sure does," said the major, glancing sharply at Johnny. "You're Indian, yourself, aren't you? Apache?"

Johnny smiled. "Cheyenne, from Wyoming," he

said. "Just the same, this kind of country feels like home to me."

The major laughed. "I guess so. Geronimo's boys came from here, and what's more they're still here. That's right; they have a big area up in the mountains just a few miles from Alamagordo, which is still their own. That's the Mescalero Apaches, you know. Been up there a couple times, and they're nice people to know today."

"Hmmm," Mike thought aloud. "Wasn't Billy the Kid from around here too?"

The major nodded. "That's right, you must have been reading about him. This is the Tularosa Basin in this section of New Mexico, with mountain ranges on both sides of it, wide desert and old graze land in the middle. Billy the Kid was shooting people up beyond the hills a ways in Lincoln county, back in the bad old days. But now all the shooting we do is rockets and atomic tests.

"Up a few dozen miles from here is Frenchman's Flat where the first atomic bomb was exploded. Tomorrow I'll take you around to the proving grounds and show you where we shot off the V-2s and the first successful American big rockets, the WAC corporals, and the rest."

"What are the white sands, and why are they called that?" asked Mike.

"You'll see. Look over to your left, way out over the desert. See that line of white just on the horizon?"

The two looked. Sure enough they could see that

faint distant white line, which they had noticed before and dismissed as evening fog or the sun's effects.

"That's the white sands. Once, a few thousand years ago, there was an inland sea filling this whole valley. When it was cut off from the ocean, it dried up slowly. As it dried up, it deposited those huge piles of white powdered gypsum in the deepest central section of this basin. The ocean is gone, but the white deposit remains—a long stretch of blinding white powder running for miles down the center of this desert."

They were coming into town now, and they were silent as the major took the car through the clean wide streets of Alamagordo, the sun lighting up the gaunt barren mountains just at the edge of town in a reddish golden glow that seemed to speak of eerie adventures and exciting promises of strange unearthly lands.

Mike thought to himself, as they drew up at a pleasant ranch-type house near the foot of the mountains, that the moon could look something like this if you were there. Gaunt mountains rising sharp and sudden from the flat unbroken treeless plain, mountains that spoke of age and bore the marks of eruptions in forgotten ages, that seemed to say to the men who looked up at them, "We are hostile to you. We suffer your presence, but refuse to bow to your rule."

Well, the mountains of the moon would be conquered someday, just as their cousins of the West had been tamed.

The car came to a halt. Mike wrenched his thoughts down to Earth and smiled as the major's wife opened the front door and two little boys in scant playsuits popped out and ran to welcome their daddy.

"Well, here we are," said Padgett. "Make yourselves at home. Tomorrow, bright and early, we go to work."

CHAPTER SIX

SONIC BOOM HIGHWAY

MIKE and Johnny and Major Padgett were standing on the cement roof of a low windowless stone building. They were looking out several hundred feet to where a single line of railroad track cut straight across the yellowish-gray desert. A little way up the track and across on the other side, Mike could make out the low cement structure of a blockhouse.

"This is it," said Major Padgett. "The world's longest captive missile track. Nine miles of absolutely straight track, hard steel rail so perfectly welded together that you can't tell where one rail ends and another begins. You're lucky to see it this morning in action."

"When do they start?" asked Mike curiously, shading his eyes against the early morning sun. They'd wasted no time this morning, he thought. Up and out at seven, a fast breakfast, and already things were in operation.

"In a few minutes," Padgett answered. "I was going to take you along to the Boeing project building and let you get the layout on the work you'll be doing here, but I figured it would be a good thing to let you see the track. It's always spectacular and it shouldn't take long."

Johnny Bluehawk peered off along the track, trying to see the end. He could make out a shape at the far end, just barely make out that something was there that glistened. That end must be four and a half miles away, but in the clear desert air it was still possible to see that something was going on.

"This is the Midway tracker building," said Padgett. "It'll pass here in full blast."

"What are they testing today?" asked Mike curiously. The sun was still low in the sky, but he could see it would be getting hot if they stood there long enough.

"Don't know what today's test is," said Padgett. "It's been stress and strain tests on missile guidance components to see how they hold up under heavy acceleration and sharp deceleration. We do a lot of that. We also have done some tests of living beings under the same stresses."

"Why," said Johnny suddenly, "this must be the same track that Colonel Stapp made his test on, when he rode to a sudden stop at several Gs pressure."

"That's right," said Padgett. "I think it's going to be soon." He pointed up the track to where a man in a green helmet had been standing by a tripod. This man was now seen to be walking rapidly away.

When the man had disappeared from view, there

was a sound of a whistle somewhere. Another whistle. "Watch sharp now," said Padgett softly.

The two astronauts stared down at the far end of the track. Suddenly there was a puff of smoke. The thing down there seemed to be moving.

With incredible speed it began to come up the track toward them. As it came there was a rising roar in the air and they saw it come racing up, then tearing past them.

They got a split-second glimpse of something silvery and red, a momentary impression of a bullet-shaped object with a long blinding tail of fiery red. The rocket sled shot past and was replaced by a rising cloud of heavy black smoke.

There was a terrific sonic boom then, and they felt the air sweep past their faces with a violent snap. A

second boom came almost on the heels of the first, and as they craned their eyes toward the other end of the track they saw the smoke abruptly end, heard a delayed whooshing sound and then sudden silence.

Johnny coughed as the black smoke swirled past him. "Phoo," he said, "Cape Canaveral was never so smoky."

"It would be if the rockets went along the ground like this one, instead of directly up," said Mike. "That one went faster than sound almost in a second. Catch that boom, and the other when it came down out of it?"

"Show's all over," said Padgett. "Let's get down. I'll tell you the full details of this track's operation a little later when you're ready for it."

As they climbed down the outside ladder of the

little building, Mike wondered aloud. "We're supposed to be fliers, to go up in rockets, not along the ground. What're you cooking up for us?"

"You'll see," said Padgett, smiling. "Let's get to our car and get on over to the place you'll be working out of for a while."

They drove in silence away from the north side of the Holloman range where the famous track was, turned, and headed for the main field and the various buildings lining it, which housed individual projects and companies working on development programs. The Boeing plant, actually a building leased to the great airplane company temporarily for the work on hand, was a long low structure, partly office building, partly hangar.

They went down a hall to the main office, entered. A couple of men stood up as they came in, and smiled at them. One was in civilian clothes, shirt sleeves rolled up, short cropped black hair betraying a college type now turned engineer.

"This is William Newbold," said Padgett. "He's chief project engineer here for the Dyna-Soar space vehicle. And this," the major added, turning to the other man, "is H. K. Serviss, who does most of the dirty work on the craft."

Serviss, who wore overalls, was a ruddy-faced, stocky blond evidently nearing forty, with all the appearance of an old hand at plane mechanics. "Hi," he said, "just call me Hack. Everyone does."

"Glad to know you," Mike said as he and Johnny

shook hands all around. "Where do we go from here?"

"Up and around the world, if you give us time," said Bill Newbold.

"And a quick, short, hard run in practically no time," said Hack. "Don't be impatient, boys. I can build 'em, but this is one I ain't going to fly."

They drew up seats around a long oblong table.

CHAPTER SEVEN

PROJECT DYNA-SOAR

"THE Dyna-Soar program is the next logical step in space flight after the X-15 and the capsule-orbited flights. It combines both projects." Bill Newbold began his discussion. He paused to look at each of his listeners.

"I don't quite get that, sir," said Johnny Bluehawk. "It seems to me that after the manned capsules the next step was to be a two-man space cabin or a more permanent spaceship type of satellite."

"Yes," said Newbold, "that's one of the next steps. But you realize that the X-15 project, which is the successful design and flight of a manned rocket-driven plane capable of operating outside the atmosphere, represented a different approach to space flight than the capsule carried on a big liquid-fuel rocket booster.

"I understand that both you and Captain Samson here—or Mike Mars, as apparently he's better known in the force—have worked with the X-15 and flown it, as a matter of fact. I've been told that you have also done a great deal of work with the space capsule launched by Redstone and Atlas rockets. This apparently makes you two the ideal men to work on a combination of both projects. For that is what Dyna-Soar is—a combination of both techniques."

"If I understand you right, you are saying that the Dyna-Soar is a sort of X-15 plane mounted on and launched by a large ballistic missile rocket," Mike said slowly. "I could imagine such a plane as being the last stage of such a rocket launching. In place of the capsule or the artificial satellite, there would be a sort of plane."

"That's it exactly," said Bill Newbold. "Dyna-Soar was conceived back in 1957 and put into the works in the following years. In 1960 and 1961 actual work began on the construction and design of its parts. To-day, now that those experimental years have passed, we can tell you that it is in an advanced stage and is almost ready for flight testing. In fact, that's why you are here."

"You're going to test-pilot the Dyna-Soar vehicle."

Mike and Johnny whistled softly.

Bill Newbold spread out some papers and diagrams on the table. "Now, follow this," he said.

"The actual plane is not the same as an X-15. That, as you know, is a true airplane driven by liquid-fuel rocket engines and launched in flight after being carried aloft and given its initial push by a B-52 bomber. The Dyna-Soar vehicle is intended to be a glider, not a plane. It will be launched as the final stage of a Titan ICBM missile, a powerful liquid-fuel rocket comparable to the Atlas and the Thor and the other big boys.

"Where the Titan would carry into space a warhead or an astronomical satellite, it will now carry this manned glider. The glider has been designed to withstand a speed of 18,000 miles an hour and reach an altitude of 300 miles. It could, as you see, go into orbit and circle the world in ninety minutes. But unlike the capsule it will be capable of controlled flight by its pilot. It can thus shift its orbit, deviate from its course, rise or descend at the will of its pilot. It can choose its own landing field and, by making a series of gliding entries into the atmosphere, come down where its pilot wills."

Johnny turned to his friend. "Say, Mike, didn't you tell me you had belonged to the glider club in your high school?"

Mike smiled. "That's right. I did fly in gliders in those days. That was before I joined the Air Force."

Hack Serviss chuckled. "They picked the right boy for this. You're going to do some fast gliding real soon. Just as soon as you can get familiar with the Dyna-Soar plane itself. When we get through here, we can go back to the hangar and take a look at it."

Mike nodded. "I'll get a kick out of that. Gosh, it's going to be something. The one thing I always felt uneasy about in space capsules is the fact that you really couldn't do anything much with it. You could slow yourself up and come down and that was it. It gave me a helpless feeling to be really just a passenger and not the actual pilot."

"You're going to have to do some fast action in this. Because our plans call for test-launching the glider here before we ever try to put it into space," said Newbold.

Major Padgett now entered the discussion. "Let me make clear what you are doing here. The Boeing Company has designed this glider, and you will see that many of the same problems encountered in the construction of the X-15 have been met by them. They have tested the plane in their plants in Colorado, have tried it out in wind tunnels and under stress conditions. But what is needed now is to test its release mechanisms at the moment of launching from the burned-out last stage of the Titan missile.

"The moment that is of greatest danger is the moment when the plane suddenly stops being just a part of the rocket and begins to enter upon its pilot-controlled flight.

"To test this, the Air Force has decided to bring the completed vehicle here and use the captive missile track. A special rocket-driven car has been constructed. The full-size Dyna-Soar glider will be attached to this in the same fashion as it will be attached to the last stage of the Titan missile. The carrier will then proceed under full blast down the track until it has reached the right momentum, at which time the pilot, riding in the glider, will release the glider and take it through the air over the proving grounds and then glide it safely down.

"You two men have been selected for this task. It's dangerous, and it's tricky, but I'm told you have the skill and guts to do it."

Mike smiled. "It should be terrific. I'm sure I can do it."

"You'd better be doubly sure," said Hack, "because if you fluff you can take that glider into the ground hard and fast at supersonic speed."

"How much time have we got?" Mike asked.

Padgett consulted a paper he had with him. "According to this, they'd like you to make your first flight test late next week. In short, you have about ten days to get completely familiar with the space glider."

"Let's not waste any more time then," said Mike. "Let's see it."

They all arose and followed the stocky mechanic out into the corridor and around the building to the back. He slid open a door, and they stepped into the cool dim interior of a hangar.

Two black-painted ships stood there on wooden blocks. Three mechanics in coveralls were working over one, going through a careful checkout of its parts.

The five men stood and looked over the plane the mechanics were not working on. Both planes were the same; again, as in the case of the X-15, the builders always kept a duplicate or triplicate plane against emergencies.

It was no longer than a standard T-38 trainer jet, but in most ways it resembled the X-15 rather than any jet plane. It was a stubby-shaped, bullet-nosed craft, whose rounded bullet front was obviously designed to withstand the resistance and pressures of a rocket launching. Narrow, thickly reinforced portholes, one at each side, and a long narrow visor-like window plate in the bulge where the pilot would be housed were the only evidence of its pilot compartment. It was straight-lined and ended abruptly, cut off sharp without a tail assemblage at all.

The most striking feature of the vehicle was its wings. "You know," said Johnny Bluehawk suddenly, "it looks for all the world like a metal version of one of those paper darts kids fold and fly around."

"You're right," said Mike. "I knew it was familiar the moment I spotted it. It has wings that slope back from the front, widen out like those of a dart. And they even fold up at the ends to form right angle tail fins for stability."

"That's it," said Newbold. "The best design for a glider is the simple old one that children have been folding out of paper for a century now. You've seen the design appear on the fastest plans for jet planes, the delta-wing planes, and this space glider is the final thing—identical. At the speed it will enter the atmosphere it should glide as smoothly as a perfect paper dart in a classroom during the teacher's absence."

They laughed. Mike walked slowly around the

plane. “I see it has vents for rockets, though,” he said. He had noticed a ring of such vents in the flat, cut-off tail, where he could also see the ends and connecting fixtures that would fasten it to the rocket launcher.

“Actually it isn’t going to rely on gliding alone,” said Major Padgett. “It will have a lot of driving power of its own in the form of solid-fuel rockets, and it will be able to maneuver in empty space by the use of these rockets. It will be able thus to speed up or to slow down at will, or to change direction, by the use of these solid-fuel blasters. I imagine that it will prove a lot easier to work with than the liquid-fuel engine of the X-15."

Mike nodded. He continued his inspection.

"No time like the present to start," said Hack Serviss. "Here're the blueprints, Captains. Let me start at once to go over this thing bolt by bolt."

CHAPTER EIGHT

ROCKET SLED RIDER

MIKE came out of the operations building the morning of his flight test wearing a jet pilot's reinforced G-suit. He was calm, as he always was on the moment of decision. There had been times during the past week and more that he had thoughts of trouble. Mike was only human, he was young, he was full of the joy of life, but for him part of that joy was the feeling of conquest of the new frontiers of space.

"Mankind has got to go out to the planets." He had once tried to explain himself to his friend Johnny. "There's no place else to go. We've explored the world. We've got to go out now and explore the universe. If we don't, the whole future of humanity becomes sealed off, like an ant colony in a container. We've got to break that container, the container of the Earth.

"We've got to be able to go out to all the stars and the worlds that God made to circle them and keep our torch of life going. Once we are out among the planets, once we are free of this world which was our egg, then humanity can never disappear. I think that's what we're meant to do. I think that's what we have got to do."

He thought of that now as he left the ops building in company with Major Padgett. Carrying his plastic helmet in one hand, on the brim of which an enterprising maintenance man had carefully lettered his initials, M.A.R.S., he walked slowly in the tight outfit, got into the waiting car.

"It's hot," said Padgett, "but I guess you can bear it for a while. We've really never had a suited pilot ride the rocket track before. We've had volunteers undergo severe acceleration, like Colonel Stapp, but they didn't need pilot's outfits."

"I'll need it now," said Mike, "though I'll probably not get too much altitude. I don't know for sure. I'll be parting from the sled at supersonic speed. I rather think I may be going to travel quite a distance before I bring the glider down."

They drove over to the end of the track. There were a cluster of helmeted men there, and the crew's derrick truck had already carried the rocket sled out and hefted it up, by hydraulic power, onto the end of the nine-mile stretch. The rocket sled was a big one, one of the biggest they had, and it had been specially rebuilt for its present task.

It was like a sled, riding on four bright red painted glistening steel slippers. Wheels would not do on such a ride. The rocket sled would slide along the tracks on its slippery skids.

It was a big thing, as large and as heavy as an

automobile, and when fully loaded it was as heavy as three such. It was slim, streamlined, and over thirty feet in length, quite the largest of the sleds at Holloman. The RS-2, as it was designated, was unusual among those sleds for being a liquid-fuel driven rocket. Usually the sleds were driven by bundles of solid-fuel rockets. This one was powered by a single-chambered rocket engine, into whose tanks men in asbestos suits were even now topping the load with additional liquid oxygen. The alcohol which would be mixed with that to form a powerful blast was already in its tanks.

Riding atop the sled, well forward, was the now-familiar black glider, attached to the rocket missile by special carriers that had been fitted to the streamlined sled for the occasion. The blunt back of the glider fitted into a flat-ended mechanism identical with what would be the top end of the final stage of a Titan missile.

It was here that the mechanisms to be tested had been installed. In actual flight, the release of the glider stage from the upper stage of the missile would be automatic. But the pilot of the glider would have the means of making the disconnection from his cockpit if he chose to do so or if for some reason he had to do so.

"During this test, the release is going to be exactly as it would be in flight," Major Padgett reminded Mike as they got out of the car at the track's end. "You've studied the problem. I think you're ready."

"Uh-huh," said Mike. "As ready as ever." He walked over to the sled. Three mechanics rolled up a scaffold on wheels. They helped him climb up it and rolled him over to the glider. A mechanic slid back the canopy, and helped Mike to climb over.

Mike settled himself down in the form-fitting pilot's seat, strapped himself in. The mechanic, leaning down, plugged in the telemetry connections. Mike knew that, as in other flight tests, his own reactions would be charted.

He squirmed a little, getting comfortable. Before him were the controls. In some respects they resembled those of the X-15, though he had no controls for liquid-fuel flight. There were, however, solid-fuel rocket controls for maneuvering in space. But this flight primarily was to be as a glider. He glanced through the thick clear narrow viewplate, and, as the mechanic pulled out and slid shut the hatch, Mike began to test his equipment.

"Pilot to blockhouse," he said. "Ready to check out."

"O.K., Mike," said Johnny's voice. "On my mark it is X minus thirty minutes."

Mike began to read off the panels and go through the careful checking. He knew where Johnny was. Johnny was in the blockhouse down near the other end of the track, at the point where they expected the glider to take off.

The blockhouse was quite different from any other he'd ever seen in that it was portable. It was an armor-plated motor-drawn trailer, containing all the telemetry and recording controls necessary. At Holloman it was driven alongside the track to the most important point, and then plugged in by cable to the intricate system of electrical controls. It was ingenious and very convenient.

Johnny Bluehawk had been assigned to the blockhouse, where he would work alongside the track control chief, the fire control engineer, Hack Serviss, and others.

Major Padgett was at the launching end of the track.

The glider, Mike knew, took a lot from the X-15. It had a similar reinforced structure. It was designed to cast off heat from re-entry and was painted the same peculiar black to resist heat as long as possible. Yet it was capable of fully sustaining life in outer space like the capsules.

As Mike continued to read off his own checkout, he could hear as a sort of background the countdown going on for the rocket sled. He knew that already all roads up to that end of Holloman were closed off. He knew that fire and ambulance equipment were ready. He knew that the many tracking stations out along the miles of desert beyond him were activated, and that radar out in King-One, the central control building, would be locating him every second.

At the moment of X minus thirty, though Mike did not see them, two yellow warning flares shot into the air, putting everyone at both ends on the alert.

"X minus twenty-five. All personnel not on duty must retire to safety."

The voice went on recounting the checkoff. Johnny and Mike completed their work. Now only the voice of the end-of-track starter was to be heard.

"X minus fifteen. Red warning." A red-colored flare arched up.

At X minus eight the igniter wires were connected to the sled.

One minute later the last track men went to safety in the pillboxes buried nearby.

"X minus five. Cameras at the ready. Everyone stand by."

Mike closed the visor of his helmet just to be on the safe side. He would have only seconds in which to work during the moment of blast-off. He couldn't risk a sudden blowout of air. He smiled slightly, rested his hands on the flight controls, watched the take-off button on his board.

"X minus one minute. Final warning!" said the voice in his ear. Somewhere beyond his sight another red flare arched up into the sky.

"X minus thirty seconds. Firing switch is unlocked," said Major Padgett's voice. Outside, everyone crouching behind cover or in the pillbox put his hands over his ears.

"Minus six . . . five . . . three . . . one . . .

"Zero!"

USAF

Mike felt himself suddenly shoved backward into his seat. In split seconds the pressure became immense, he felt himself being crushed intolerably. He strained his muscles to hold control.

Outside there was a terrific roar, a blast that rocked back and forth across the landscape, that thundered about everyone's ears. There was an outpouring of violent eye-searing yellow-orange flame, which almost instantly stretched out to become a mile-long plume of fire racing down the track.

Johnny Bluehawk saw the sudden outburst of smoke, got a momentary impression of fire, then at a speed that outpaced the sound there was a split-second vision of a black batlike thing mounted on a gleaming scarlet bullet coming along the steel road, there was a sudden impression of coming apart, and he saw the black batlike thing, the glider meant for outer space, break away from the red rocket sled and hurtle across the landscape and vanish over the horizon, rising momentarily in the distant blue sky and vanishing somewhere in the faint haze of the distant desert.

Then the sound caught up with the blockhouse and its thunder mingled with the terrific sonic boom that blasted from nearby, outside.

CHAPTER NINE

DYNA ONE: EVERYTHING IS GO!

PERHAPS it was fortunate for Mike that the actual moment of launching was automatic. For though his hand did press down on the disconnect button the moment his eye registered the yellow flash on his controls that signaled the burnout of the rocket, it is possible that even the time it took for him to spot it might have been disastrous.

Were this a case where the glider was being launched from the last stage of a burned-out missile, the situation would have been much easier. For in that case, the actual rocket ride would not have taken just a few seconds from start to finish but would have taken enough time for him to prepare himself mentally for the moment of action.

In both cases, of course, he would have been crushed under heavy acceleration, so that the G-forces in him would have multiplied his body weight many times. In a missile launching he would have had this pressure come upon him more slowly. In the sled launching it was terribly sudden—and the release was just as sharp.

He had felt himself shoved back with unusual violence. He had, in the past, ridden the centrifuges in testing areas and had learned how much pressure he could stand. Here it came with a blow like the slap of a giant's fist.

He had struggled for an instant to keep from blacking out. He saw through narrowed eyes the sudden rushing forward of the landscape. He had a few seconds' impression of the rails swirling beneath him, of the ground on both sides rushing past; then the moment of decision, the plane shooting forward pointing itself upward in a slow rising angle, and within seconds more he was alone in the blue sky, sitting released in sudden silence.

He grasped the controls, swept a practiced eye over his dials. He was traveling faster than sound, though his strange glider was traveling as a bullet travels, on the momentum of its initial charge. Like a model plane slung from a rubber band, he thought to himself. He was rising steadily, rising into the air, a mile, two miles high, more.

The plane was losing speed slowly. He became aware of the faint hum in his ears—the radio was still on. Then a voice, Johnny's voice, "Dyna One, calling Dyna One. This is Tracker. How's it going?"

"A-O.K., Tracker," Mike sung out. "Everything's Go! How'd it look?"

"Terrific, Mike," said Johnny. "What a take-off! Where are you now?"

Mike glanced at his controls, then leaned forward, peered out. He could see the sky like a blue bowl,

cloudless. He could see far off the blunted barren teeth of mountains and below the yellowish level of the desert, with here and there a streak of brilliant white. He strained his eyes, saw at last a cluster of tiny lines far off to one side, near the mountains.

"Can't quite tell," Mike called. "I see a town, passing by fast to my left. My reading, Mach one point three and dropping."

"Tracker to Dyna One," cut in another voice. Padgett, Mike thought. "That may be Tularosa. Try bringing her around."

"Can do," said Mike. He settled back. The glider was traveling fast and high now; it was time to test the controls.

He swung it around; the rudders set upright on the dartlike wings operated in good order. Nothing damaged—the builders had worked well. The black arrowhead ship swung around in a turn that covered miles. Then he was moving back through the sky, heading south now. In seconds he saw the configuration of Holloman show up far below, then disappear behind him.

For over forty minutes Mike kept the glider up, for it sped through the high air with wonderful smoothness, and its initial speed had been greater, he thought, than any glider that had ever been launched before in flying history. It was smooth; in some ways he found it smoother than the X-15, for that craft had had less wing space and had been handicapped by the presence of too much tank space and a heavy rocket engine.

He tried the rockets briefly. A spurt on one wing and the glider spun around, a spurt on the other side balanced it. Then he slowly allowed the ship to lose altitude while waiting for the speed to diminish to the point where he could attempt a landing.

He soared the length and breadth of the great White Sands Proving Grounds and at times he could see El Paso in the distance or, on the northern swing, that curious patch of glazed ground where the first atomic tests had been held many many years ago.

Then he prepared for his descent. Closer and closer to the runway at Holloman he came, swooping and swinging, while his black dart lost speed. He announced his decision to land, saw the tiny dots that were emergency trucks and crew men clear the field.

He came down, fired his forward retro-rockets. The glider seemed to buck, seemed to pull back in air, his speed fell sharply, and he came closer. Off with the rockets, one more swing around, he thought.

"I'm coming in," he announced at last. "South to North."

He came around now, the ground close. He could see the desert, a clump of tough brush every now and then breaking it. Here was the runway. He lowered himself, speed still perilously high for a landing he thought, but he was committed. He couldn't attempt another swing.

Lower and lower, and then with a bump he felt the skids connect. The Dyna-Soar glider had followed the example of the X-15 by being equipped with skids rather than wheels.

There was a cloud of dust being plowed up on

both sides. Oddly enough, his thought was, the field crew is going to be mad. I'm ruining their runway.

Then the tail of his glider came down, its skid touched, there was another cloud of dust, and the glider slid screamingly to a stop.

He took his hands off the controls, drew a breath. He reached up, opened the hatch. He heard the sirens of the ambulance and the fire trucks coming up on him, and distantly some cheering.

He unbuckled his belt, stood up. Running across the field were a group of men. He recognized Johnny and Hack Serviss. He waved to them.

"Everything apple pie," he shouted. "Bring on your Titan missiles!"

CHAPTER TEN

ONE OF OUR ASTRONAUTS IS MISSING

THE successful completion of the test did not end the day's work for Mike and Johnny—far from it. For they put in a busy afternoon at the works building discussing the test, checking through the tapes, and assisting the mechanics who were carefully going over the glider to find out what, if any, damage had been done.

So it was late in the afternoon when the two young astronauts were able to get away. They found Major Padgett waiting for them in his car.

"Instead of eating dinner at home, I'm giving the wife a rest from us," the major said. "I'm taking you two over to the Officers' Club. There's someone there waiting for us."

Mike and Johnny exchanged glances. They wondered who that was. But when the three fliers walked into the dining area of the sprawled-out clubhouse, Mike spotted their visitor.

"Why it's Colonel Drummond!" he said, and sure enough it was. The military director of Space Task Group Q was there ahead of them, holding down a table for four.

It was soon evident during the meal that Major Padgett had been briefed in secret on the remarkable achievements of their astronautic crew. For Drummond did not seem to be afraid to discuss what was going on back at Skyhook and at Canaveral in his presence.

"What are the plans for Stacey's flight?" asked Mike after he became sure that it was all right to talk about it in front of Padgett. It was always wonderful to him how well Air Force officers could keep private those important defense operations where secrecy was required. At Holloman all sorts of important advanced projects were tested, and he realized that the major was in a position where many of these would be known to him. During the days they had stayed with Padgett and his family, he had not uttered a word to indicate any knowledge of their capsule orbiting, yet he had known all along.

"Stacey will be sent into orbit next Monday," the colonel said. "We plan this time to have him remain at least forty-eight hours in orbit, and if everything goes well we may extend that another day. We have arranged for air and water purification for at least five days at the utmost and we will stock enough food for that same length of time."

"That will make things kind of crowded in the capsule," said Mike. "There never was much room to begin with."

"To do it, we have to rearrange some of the equip-

The facet-eye camera

ment, but we managed to work it out," was Drummond's answer.

"Where do we come in on this?" asked Mike.

"We've got a minor assignment for you two here. I'm out here to work with you on both this and your own work. Padgett, here, is directing your Dyna-Soar testing, but I'm to try later on to talk NASA into letting one of you attempt a full-fledged Dyna-Soar mission from Cape Canaveral, launching you from a Titan missile. Both Martin and Boeing, who built the project, are willing. If I decide it's ripe, it may then come off in a couple months."

"That'll be exciting," said Mike. "I hope you can."

Drummond nodded. "However, the immediate task in connection with Stacey's orbit is to be your job next Monday. I will be at the telemetry station here at Holloman, checking Stacey through as he comes over each lap. But you two will be attempting to take a picture of his capsule as he comes past."

"What!" said both fellows in unison. "How do we do that?" came in Mike's voice. "With a camera?" was Johnny's query.

Padgett laughed, and answered for the colonel. "We've got a camera here that can take pictures of satellites in orbit as they go past. We've got quite a lot of those pictures—in fact, I think we may have one or two of certain capsules containing certain young aviators I know quite well. So on Monday you'll be with me over at the facet-eye installation out at its astrodome in the North Area. It's quite a device. You'll get a kick out of it!"

"That sounds like fun," said Mike. "It'll give us the feeling of being on the spot. I'd have been sorry not to have seen Stacey take off."

"How's Joe looking?" Johnny asked the colonel.

"Oh, he's fit as a fiddle," said Drummond. "We're going to let him take the day off Sunday again. You know Dr. Holderlin's orders. No worrying about a flight the day before. I understand Vivian has talked him into going over to one of the lakes and trying some fishing."

The week went past quickly enough. Time always moves when you are engaged in work, and progress on the Dyna-Soar occupied time. Besides, the boys took time off to check in and watch some of the other interesting things going on at the Air Force Missile Development Center—and what with the testing of smaller missiles, work on the rocket track, a balloon ascension at the field's stratosphere section offices, they managed to keep themselves interested.

On Sunday, Mike and Johnny and the Padgett family went on an outing in the mountains.

That same Sunday, hundreds of miles to the east, in central Florida, Joe Stacey left to go fishing. Vivian had intended to go along, but the day before she had received an unexpected invitation to a sorority party at the home of one of her friends on Sunday, and as it promised to be fun, she didn't want to miss it. So Vivian begged out of the date. She made it up to Joe by offering him the use of her speedy red sports car for his trip. Joe was delighted to get the use of her car.

So off he went by himself with his rod and reel, a nice assortment of flies, a can of bait, and a basket lunch in the bucket seat next to him. But he didn't return for supper that night.

He telephoned Skyhook a couple of hours after dark. He'd had car trouble. He'd driven rather deep into the fairly isolated area of small lakes and swamps, had done some nice fishing, and had started back along a narrow, little-used rural road all overgrown with vines and Spanish moss when the engine of Vivian's car had suddenly conked out.

He'd spent two hours practically taking the engine apart to find out what was wrong. By then it had gotten dark, but he'd found the spot—the cylinder head was cracked and would have to be replaced. It proved to be a long walk in the dark before he located a house with a phone.

"As soon as I can locate a repair station with a tow truck that will come out here, I'll start back. I can't just ditch the car in the road. I'll have to stick with it until it's safely garaged and they can start to fix it. I'll try to be back by midnight," he told Dr. Van Ness over the phone.

The director shook his head. "I suppose you can catch up with your sleep during the orbiting," he commented. "But don't strain yourself, and try to get here as soon as possible."

He hung up, and tried to shake off his feeling of unease. Joe wasn't going to find any replacement parts for that foreign-made sports car in any hurry. Not in those parts, certainly. He regretted not having pulled his rank and ordered Joe to return at once regardless of the car's trouble. Unfortunately there was no way of calling Joe back.

At seven o'clock in the morning, Jack Lannigan was up and the two directors soon joined him. But Joe Stacey had not returned.

CHAPTER ELEVEN

SILENCE IN SPACE

"THE countdown is proceeding. The count is now T minus eighty-five minutes," said the voice of the talker.

All around the blockhouse men were quietly proceeding about their work. In the three television screens up on the wall could be seen the image of an Atlas rocket on its pad, with wisps of haze circling its base. The wisps were evidence of its condition—it was already fueled with liquid oxygen, though it was still connected, and men in protective suits and metal helmets clustered around it.

At the back of the blockhouse, where they would not interfere with the work of the countdown, stood Dr. Van Ness and astronaut Jack Lannigan. The bearded scientist was plainly worried.

"You say Stacey called in an hour ago that he was on his way," he said to the lanky young man with him. "He ought to be here by now. If he doesn't show up in another twenty-five minutes, I'm going to have to put a hold on the count."

Lannigan shifted uneasily, pounded one hand on the other. "It wasn't Stacey himself that called in," he said. "According to the man who answered the call at Skyhook, it was a garageman who called in. He said they had not got the car repaired but that Joe was being driven here fast by a neighbor."

"Well," said Van Ness, "Joe will still have to get into his outfit, and that will take time. I don't like it. He's likely to be under condition—tired or nervous."

"Hope not," said Jack. "Joe's a pretty calm boy. Besides when Dr. Holderlin gets a look at him, he'll be able to judge. The doctor is waiting for him at the central control building, isn't he?"

"Sure," said Van Ness. "He was going to be at the telemetry station at Patrick, but with this delay, he wants to be able to supervise Joe's dressing for the trip in person."

They stood quietly for a while, watching the proceedings. Out on the pad, the big red gantry was still in place, waiting for the astronaut who would go up to its top level and climb into the waiting capsule.

Steadily the countdown went on. It got to seventy, then to sixty-five. Dr. Van Ness bit his lip, waited tensely. At sixty-one, he'd call to the talker and at sixty he'd bring the whole count to a halt.

It wasn't good business at this stage. Because even under perfectly ordinary natural conditions there were often enough holds on such a countdown. If the weather changed a little, if a strange plane wandered into the Canaveral area, if something registered a little off on the elaborate series of checks on the

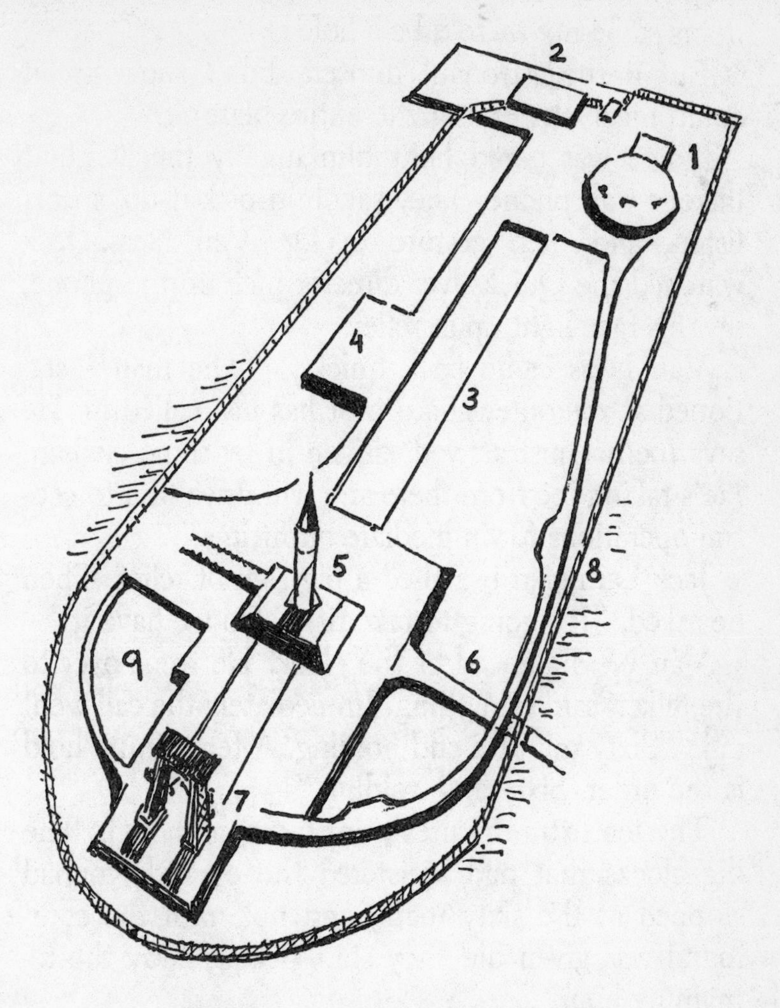

TYPICAL MISSILE LAUNCH SITE

1. Blockhouse
2. Ready room
3. Water main
4. Fuel storage
5. Ramp and test stand area
6. Drainage
7. Service tower
8. Security fence
9. Fuel storage

mighty liquid-fuel rocket, if any of dozens of tiny items came up, there'd be a hold.

But if the astronaut himself didn't show up, it could mean the end of the entire blast-off.

There was a red light blinking by the assistant talker's wall phone. They saw him pick it up, speak, listen, and then gesture to Dr. Van Ness. Jack watched the Quicksilver director pick up the phone, saw his face light up in relief.

Van Ness came back quickly. "The man I stationed at the outer guard post has just called in. He says Joe has just arrived, driven in by some civilian. He's taking Joe from there and will drive him to central operations for immediate outfitting."

Jack Lannigan breathed a big sigh of relief. Then he asked, "It's going to take time. Do we have it?"

Van Ness glanced at the clock. He went over to the talker, said something. Immediately the call went out: "Sixty minutes and holding. A ten-minute hold is the order. Sixty and holding."

The ten extra minutes went by soon enough. The big clocks that had registered the countdown had stopped at the sixty mark, and not until the command was given did they start ticking away the remaining hour.

Then at last the hold was lifted and the countdown proceeded past sixty and down toward the moment, now less than an hour away, when Joe Stacey would blast off into an orbital flight that might set a new record for America.

Van Ness and Jack, without any word necessary, went out of the blockhouse, through the thick doorway that could block the direct hit of a cannon shell, and stood just outside.

In a few minutes a yellow-painted van came along, drove on up the ramp to the foot of the great gantry. Two technicians jumped down from it, opened a side door, and helped a strange figure out.

The figure was clad in shining silver, the mark of the special pressure suit worn by the astronauts. His wide plastic helmet was already on, visor closed and sealed into the suit's internal ventilation system. Following the astronaut out of the van came the gray-haired figure of Dr. Holderlin, and the two of them—the astronaut and the space doctor—went to the elevator and slowly rose story after story to the top of the great framework.

Jack and Van Ness could see distantly the silvery figure being helped into the capsule, and finally saw Holderlin and the technicians with him return to the elevator. This was the signal for the two on the ground to go back into the blockhouse.

"I wish Joe had arrived earlier," said Van Ness. "I doubt if Holderlin had time to give him much more than a quick checkover. I wonder if he got any sleep?"

Jack frowned slightly. "T minus forty-three and counting," said the talker's voice.

They watched. As the countdown proceeded, there came the checkoffs for the suit and the capsule.

Joe Stacey's voice seemed clear and calm enough as he gave the responses to the routine questions. Everything seemed to be functioning.

"Readings for pulse and respiration rate for the astronaut are a little high," said Lannigan slowly.

"Not surprising," said the other, "considering the rush and the circumstances. He'll be up there long enough to normalize, I'm sure. We'll arrange a nap for him in a couple hours."

The countdown went on. Everything was going perfectly. Finally the last few moments were reeling off. Outside the horns had cleared away everyone, the gantry had rolled away, the Atlas was held up by a single beam, and a few connections only held it to the Earth. Then these were snapped, the count went on, the high rocket stood alone, covered with frost and fuming with its powerful fuels.

Then it was ten seconds, and nine, and down and down, and two, one, then zero. The Atlas seemed to hesitate a moment, to fight against the sudden flush of blinding flame that poured from its base. Then slowly, in a terrible earth-shattering roar, it began to rise.

Up and up it went and the beam fell over and away and it moved faster and then it seemed to speed up, and finally it was away, moving into the sky like a blazing arrow right into the heavens.

There was a period then of uncertainty, of suspense, while everyone waited to know if the capsule would release on schedule, if nothing would go

wrong. The checkers watched, and the reports came in.

The capsule was releasing, it was released; it was performing a flip-flop into space; it was in orbit; it was going right.

There was a moment, a bad moment, of uncertainty for one second. The flip-flop seemed slightly off. One of the automatic little rockets in the capsule that would turn it on course seemed a little delayed. The error was slight, but it seemed to have been corrected.

Again a wait. Then a call from the telemetry building at Great Bahama station. "Capsule recorded overhead on schedule. Definitely in orbit."

There was a brief cheer from the men in the blockhouse. The waiting was over, everything had gone right after all. The men stood up, crowded around the talker, asking further details from the telemetry reports.

"Any word from the astronaut?" asked Van Ness suddenly. "Has Stacey reported in?"

Nobody knew. Dr. Van Ness rang Holderlin at the telemetry station at Patrick Air Force Base. He spoke a moment.

"They have not spoken to Stacey," he said, hanging up. "Their readings show pulse and respiration a little slow. They think he may be stunned, momentarily unconscious. They're trying to raise him now."

Jack Lannigan frowned. "That's not like Joe. He's a pretty sturdy boy. I'm surprised."

But Merlin Van Ness bit his lips and ran a hand through his short beard. "I'm afraid that I was too anxious to get this test started. I had no business letting Joe go up in low physical condition. I should have set this whole flight back twenty-four hours, or replaced the astronaut with you, Lannigan."

"Oh, come, sir, let's not be hasty with our judgments. Suppose we drive up to Patrick and join Dr. Holderlin. By that time, we should have news." Jack tried to reassure the director, but he didn't feel as confident as he tried to make his voice sound.

CHAPTER TWELVE

THE BUG-EYED SPY

THE morning of an orbited flight was always one of special excitement to Mike and Johnny. This Monday was no exception. They were up bright and early, and out at Holloman at the beginning of operations, even though the Atlas at faraway Cape Canaveral was not going to be something they could observe.

"Every step," as Mike said to Johnny during the drive across the North Area of the great desert testing range, "is important. Everything learned, and every day we learn it, is another inch toward taking man into outer space."

"That's right," said Johnny. "Keep on taking tiny steps, and they will lead to sudden big steps. One day we will be on the moon and full of impatience just to get out further and see what is doing on the sands of Mars."

"That's the ticket," said Mike. "First orbit, then the moon, then probably Venus, and at last Mars. We'll do it, too."

"But right now," said Padgett, who had been listening quietly, "you'll just be looking. Here's the observatory."

The two young fellows looked at the structure they were drawing up to. It looked like an astronomical observatory—the small kind one sees sometimes on college campuses. It was a circular building, with a large rounded dome. The dome was slit and at this time open wide; through it they saw a curious series of barrels projecting.

"It doesn't look like any telescope I ever saw," said Mike. "It looks like a multibarreled anti-aircraft gun, the kind they used before the ground-to-air rocket was put into effect."

"It does, doesn't it?" agreed Major Padgett. "There are twenty-five of those metal barrels, all clustered together and all pointing in the same direction. But they are not gun barrels, they are telescopes. Each barrel is a five-inch refracting telescope, and they move together and are directed together with one set of controls."

"Hmmm," Mike said slowly. "Unusual. I don't see quite how it is supposed to work."

They got out of the car and looked up at the telescope cluster. Then they went inside.

Here they found three young men at work. The inside of the observatory again did not resemble Mike's ideas of such a place. He thought he would see someone perched upon a stool looking into a lens, or at least directing a lens into a photographic plate. What he came into was a small chamber which at first looked quite a lot like the telemetry station, with five high banks of panels covered with dials, meters,

W. E. Woehl, originator of the facet-eye camera

and plug-in connections. At one side of the room was a console, with a TV-type screen, and one of the young men was sitting before this, watching a series of bright lights swish across it, while the other two were at the panels manipulating controls at his direction.

Padgett stood quietly until the man at the controls looked up. He switched off the machine and everyone relaxed. Introductions were made. Then Mike insisted on learning what everything was.

"We call it a facet-eye camera, because it uses a whole group of tiny eyes to make one big seeing apparatus," Major Padgett said.

"I know where I remember that word from," Mike

suddenly said. "The multiple eyes of insects are called facet-eyes!"

"Right!" said the major. "That's the principle we use here. Instead of one giant lens, we have put together twenty-five small telescopes. Looking in the same direction at the same time, each registers a view of a small part of the sky. All together they cover a larger segment of the sky than any single telescope. Now see how this works." He pointed around as he demonstrated.

"The images from each small telescope are received on individual television screens. These in turn transmit the combined twenty-five images to one main viewing plate, so that what comes out is not twenty-five separate little pictures, but one great picture. This can be viewed with the naked eye, or it can be photographed, which brings into even clearer view what we are looking at."

"The advantage of this facet-eye camera," said the technician who had been at the main viewer, "is that it can actually see stars in the daytime. This observatory is the only one in the world which can view the sky at any time of night or day and get results. The facet-eye system was designed primarily for looking at passing space satellites, and it works. We can train it at the part of the sky where satellites will be—and even though they're invisible to the naked eye and a single big telescope could not likely find them, we can get them. Further, we can see them so exactly that we can take clear photos of the satellite itself, just as if we were up close to it."

"What you boys will watch is the capsule that will be orbiting from Canaveral in just a little time now," said Padgett. "I'll leave you now, because I'm joining Drummond at NASA's telemetry station here. So keep a sharp eye, boys, and maybe your friend will wave to you as he goes past."

"That I have to see," said Mike, laughing.

During the next hour, the two were shown over the remarkable observatory, and looked over many of the amazing photographs that had been taken. One they recognized as either Mike's or Johnny's, but they did not attempt to identify it too clearly since they were not sure whether the observatory men knew exactly who they were.

The photos were clear, remarkably so. They could see the capsule, and could even distinguish faintly the letters that identified it as U. S. Air Force.

The phone rang. It was for Mike. "Take-off in five minutes," said Drummond's voice. "If everything goes on schedule, you can expect to try for a view in a little over an hour. We'll keep in touch by phone."

"Very good, sir," said Mike. "We're ready here."

They waited while the facet-eye operators went back to their posts and began slowly sweeping the sky. Mike and Johnny stood behind the console operator, watching the unexpected appearance on this marvelous screen of stars and planets they knew were up there in the bright blue sunlit sky. But thanks to

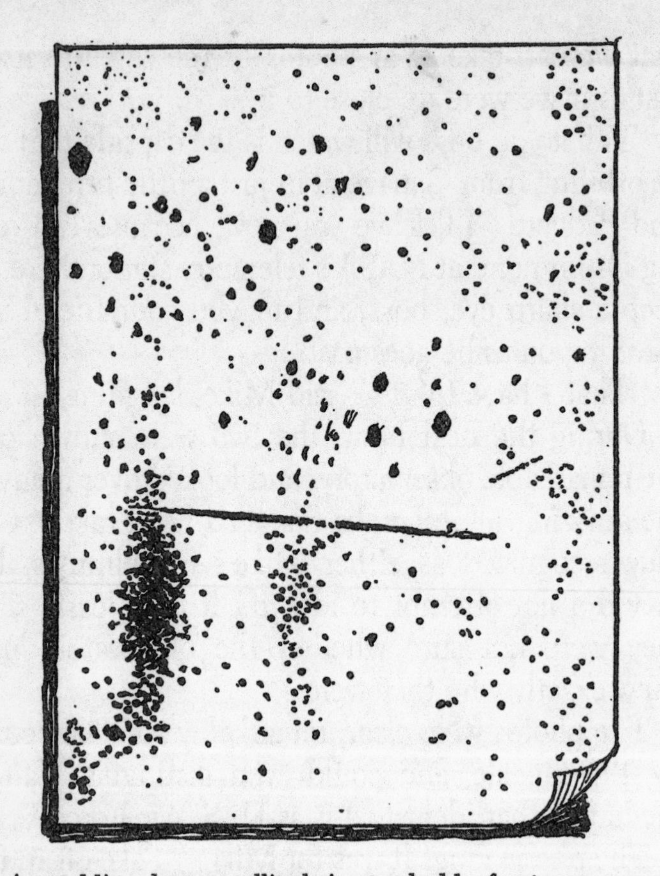

Horizontal line shows satellite being tracked by facet-eye camera

the magic of TV-plus-telescope-plus-electronics they were made visible.

They kept an eye on the clock, and after five minutes they glanced at each other. In their minds' eyes they could see the Atlas slowly rising, with Joe Stacey forced down in his contour seat within the nose enclosure, fighting his way against G-pressures into space.

Five more minutes. Then ten, then fifteen. Another hour and they'd be watching for it. Then the phone rang.

Mike picked it up. Drummond was on the phone. Johnny glanced at him, and saw Mike's face suddenly change; Mike seemed surprised. The Cheyenne drew himself up, went over.

Mike whistled, then hung up and turned around. Quickly he told Johnny what had happened at Canaveral.

"Van Ness is really worried. So far there's been no word from Stacey, and whether he's injured or just knocked out is uncertain."

Johnny was silent at the news. Then finally he said, "We'll just have to wait and see. There's bound to be some word."

Word from the capsule did not come until a half hour more of tension, as tracking station after tracking station on the links around the world called in their readings as the satellite came within each one's range. Each time the readings showed the astronaut to be still unconscious. But at last there was better news.

Joe Stacey had come to. His pulse reading was up. His respiration showed normal breathing. His temperature was normal. Joe had survived after all. But the question remained—what had happened?

It was the NASA tracking station at Woomera, in the Great Australian Desert, that was the first to speak with the new satellite. Orin McMahan, on duty there, made the routine calls and he was answered.

A little hesitantly Joe explained to Orin that somehow he had had a jolt when the capsule flip-flopped into orbital position. He admitted that he'd only been able to catch a few hours' sleep the night before. He'd gotten to a garage after it was closed. It had taken time to get the owner to open up. He hadn't been able to get a car to take him further until dawn.

That was the news that Orin relayed halfway around the world. Drummond telephoned it to Mike as soon as he had heard it.

"He says Joe now sounds all right and says he will continue with the mission," said Mike, hanging up and turning to his Cheyenne friend.

"That's a big relief," said Johnny. "It won't be too long before Joe comes by overhead. Let's get back on telescope duty."

"Yes," said Mike, "and let's hope everything stays all right. Drummond says that Doc Van Ness is still quite upset about the whole thing and thinks he shouldn't have let Joe go up."

CHAPTER THIRTEEN

VISION OF DOOM

If Merlin Van Ness was nervous, he was trying hard not to show it. But he wasn't fooling the keen medical eye of Dr. Holderlin. Van Ness was shaken up by the whole episode and seemed determined to shoulder the blame himself.

"At least," he said to the space-medicine expert, "it seems to have come out all right. We should order Joe to go into rest in another hour or so, and thereby get back some of his energy."

"So?" said Holderlin. "But we cannot do that yet. We must first wait until we see whether he becomes spacesick. If he is in low condition, that should be even sooner than it took Bluehawk. Maybe, also, keeping awake will serve to remind him not to take chances just before such an important mission."

Van Ness nodded. He was still uneasy. His feeling was going to be more than justified as the day went on.

Stacey's capsule passed across the wide Pacific, crossed over California, and began to traverse the southwestern desert states. On the edge of New Mexico, at the White Sands Proving Grounds, the twenty-five eyes of the unique observatory peered into the sky at the point where the new satellite should first appear.

Mike watched in silence as the operators scanned the viewer, waiting for the first indication of the capsule's crossing. Then a word from one of the men at the panel and a click as he pressed an automatic trigger that would lock the facet-eye camera telescope on its target and keep moving with it across the sky. "Object in view!"

Mike and Johnny stood close behind the man at the seat of the main viewing console and watched. They saw at first a blurry object begin to cross the glowing field of the television-camera screen. Then, with careful manipulation by the operator's deft fingers, the blur was caught and held in the center of the screen and rapidly began to expand. It shimmered in and out, it flickered like a poor TV reception, then it suddenly clarified.

They could see now that it was the capsule. They could see the dark metal of it and catch a slight flickering where the sun bounced off it. There were instances when it was sharp and moments when Mike almost felt he could see the markings on it.

They kept it in view as it crossed over. The two astronauts knew also that a photographic record was being made of the object and that among the photos there would be prints sharp enough to see all they needed to see.

In a few minutes the capsule had passed overhead

and vanished from the scope of their bug-eyed machine. The phone buzzed and Johnny answered. It was Drummond at the telemetry station.

"Stacey is now in high spirits," he said. "He says he was knocked out by the take-off, says the capsule jolted sort of hard as it flip-flopped into orbital position and that put him out, coming as it did on top of the intense pressures of the acceleration."

Johnny reported the conversation to Mike, who shook his head. "Overenthusiasm can be a bad sign, too, you know. I wonder if the oxygen supply isn't getting him a bit high—too much oxygen in the air can make you sort of lightheaded and acting a little drunk."

"I imagine they'd know that at telemetry," said Johnny. "When are we going to see those pictures?"

"Give me another few minutes, boys," said the chief technician. "They're developing now automatically."

They waited the required time, and then the photos were ready. Large and still damp, they were laid out on a flat table just outside the control chamber, and everyone crowded around. Many of the shots were blurs, but there were a half dozen brilliantly clear close-ups of the capsule. They were almost as clear as if they had been taken from about thirty feet away while the capsule was standing still in the sun.

"Terrific!" exclaimed Johnny. "I can read the lettering, see all the details."

"Pity you can't see inside," said Mike. "I wonder

if Joe is really as well off as he sounds." He picked up one of the photos and studied it, then picked up each of the other clear ones and scanned them. His eyes hardened, he hastily looked again at the first one, then laid several down side by side and looked quite troubled.

"What's the matter, Mike?" asked Johnny. "See something?"

"I'm afraid so," said Mike slowly. "Look at this and then compare it with this. Does this look quite right to you?"

The two photos were not exactly the same, for they were taken as the capsule was moving and as different parts of it came into view. Mike's finger pointed now to a section of the wide end of the top-shaped capsule. This was the end just behind the back of the astronaut's seat, the end which would re-enter the atmosphere first when the time came.

The flattened end bulged out into the wide canister containing the impact absorption mechanism, and also concealed the small retro-rockets that would operate to slow down the capsule so that it would begin its re-entry.

"There seems to be a dent here," said Mike, indicating the spot on the photo. "And it seems to me that there is an area where several bolts are either off or twisted. Here's the vent for one of the retro-rockets, and the way this is now warped it looks to me that its blast will brush against the impact skirt container."

“Unless there’s some way to rescue Joe, he’s doomed.”

Johnny whistled softly as he examined Mike's discovery. "If this is so," he said in a hushed tone, "Joe's not going to be able to make a successful re-entry. When that rocket fires, it's going to crack or ignite the shock pad. Besides, it's out of alignment. It will start the capsule whirling as it comes down."

"That's right," said Mike, his face suddenly pale. "There was reference to some sort of jolt or jerking motion at the time of the capsule's release from the burned-out Atlas. This must have been when it happened. Something failed to disconnect quickly enough."

Johnny and he were silent for a few moments. The facet-eye technicians looked at them gravely, aware that something was seriously amiss.

"I'd say, Johnny," Mike finally commented, hating even to say the words, "that he's not going to be able to make a successful return to Earth. If they try to start the re-entry maneuvers, this capsule is going to crack and then burn up as it comes down."

The two looked at each other, then Mike silently turned, went to the phone, rang Drummond.

"What's going to happen?" the chief technician whispered to Johnny as Mike was explaining his discovery to the colonel.

The Cheyenne shook his head, his face impassive. "Unless there's some way to rescue him, Joe's doomed."

CHAPTER FOURTEEN

DYNA-SOAR EMERGENCY

"COME ON," said Mike, gathering up the photos, "Colonel Drummond wants to see these and to hold a conference. Let's not waste any time getting over there."

With the photos under his arm, the two fellows waved a quick good-by to the men at the facet-eye astrodome and scooted out. In only a few minutes, they were driven over to the big windowless radar and telemetry building known as King-One, which was the center of all Holloman tracking activities. The car pulled up, the boys jumped out and in a few more minutes were seated with Colonel Drummond and Major Padgett at a table in a small consulting room, poring again over the pictures.

Reluctantly Drummond agreed with Mike's estimate. "To attempt to start these rockets would be a disaster. Maybe Stacey might be able to scrape through the violent and jagged re-entry—by maneuvering or shifting."

Johnny's dark eyes stared at the pictures. He slowly shook his head. "Whatever is to be done, an astronaut can't do it. There's too much repair involved. His chances of coming down are very small. But maybe that's the only thing that can be attempted. The controls can be directed from Canaveral—Van Ness will have to start them and hope Joe will survive the crash."

Mike and Drummond looked at each other. "Not really any chance of that," Mike said. "No one can expect Van Ness to attempt it. It'd be only one chance in a hundred for Joe's life."

Major Padgett coughed slightly. "I'm not really up on all this but isn't there some way someone can go up and save him? How about another capsule sent up in another Atlas? Then the two getting together?"

Drummond shook his head. "To launch another capsule would take too long. We've no Atlas on the pad now, and it would be at least a week before we could get one up, check it down, ready a capsule. Then there's the matter of what we call rendezvous in space. The two bodies must meet—and that means they must arrive together at the same height and the same speed. The capsules are not equipped for delicate maneuvers. Except for their ability to slow down and make re-entry, they're little more than helpless satellites."

Mike looked up then. "There is a way," he said. "We have a ship that can maneuver in space, and the means of launching it in time. The Dyna-Soar project! We have the glider—it works, it's tested. We only need the Titan launching missile and there must be some available. We have only to get the glider over to such a missile, attach it, and figure the time and direction of launching."

"Yes," said Johnny Bluehawk as soon as Mike stopped. "Mike could do it. He's flown the glider and he's flown the X-15 in space, too. Why not let him try it?"

The colonel sat back, thinking it over. Slowly he shook his head. "I can't see it. The thing's still not tested fully. How can we risk your life, too, on such a thing?"

Major Padgett also shook his head. "We were not expected to try a real Dyna-Soar launching for at least another year. We have many tests to make on this glider—even though it seems to be in working order. We have never had a trial with the rocket-launching missile and the glider together."

Mike now became enthusiastic. He turned to them and began to argue with increased feeling. They could risk it, he said. The glider worked. Sure, it wasn't perfect, but it was complete and the flight would be a good test. It could be glided back without trouble no matter what happened. Let him try it—somehow Stacey must be rescued.

As the colonel continued to shake his head, Johnny spoke up. "Look, sir, the whole point and purpose of Space Task Group Q is to cut corners, to win time for America in the space race. You mustn't forget that we are all volunteers who are expendable. If we can cut a whole year from the

Dyna-Soar's success this is worth the risk of any of our lives. Let *me* go—I've not flown in the glider, but it's my turn and it's my life."

Drummond's features tensed. "The only person who could go is the only person who actually flew the thing—and would have the best chance of mastering it. That's Mike. But you're right—you're not supposed to be kept in cotton wrappings. I'm going to call Van Ness and Holderlin."

There was a phone in the room, and in a few more minutes Drummond was on the wire speaking to Dr. Van Ness. Rapidly he explained the situation and Mike's suggestion. There seemed to be some hesitancy, some disagreement. Finally the boys heard him address Holderlin, as Van Ness turned his end of the call over to his associate.

For ten minutes the boys sat in tense silence as the directors argued for and against the effort. Finally Drummond hung up, took out a handkerchief, and mopped his brow. Though the building King-One was perfectly air-conditioned, he was perspiring heavily.

"Holderlin agrees with us. He consents. Van Ness says he will go along with the majority. Holderlin is going to call headquarters in Washington and try to get an O.K. on it. It will involve a lot of red tape, I'm afraid."

They all sat back, wrapped in thought. Finally they all stood up. "Let's see what's new about the

capsule," remarked Mike, and they went out and into the main telemetry room.

The men at the various consoles were sitting quietly back. The capsule was on the outer side of the Earth at the time and there was nothing much to do. They talked in whispers with the operators.

Reports were favorable. Stacey's radio comments to the various stations showed good spirits and good health so far. He had been given no hint of the desperate problem he faced.

"Holderlin is even going ahead with his physical tests to offset spacesickness," commented Drummond in a low voice. "Joe will be taking the first anti-nausea pills soon. Later on, in an hour or so, he'll be asked to sleep and eat."

They returned to the consultation room. Drummond rang back to Canaveral. "Still no final word," they heard him say to whomever had answered. "Yes, we'll go ahead and make plans anyway. Right . . . Right . . . Call SAC headquarters and Colorado Springs. . . . Will do."

He hung up. "Headquarters at NASA are trying to get permission from the Air Force chiefs at the Pentagon for the effort. There are Titan missiles set up at several Strategic Air Command bases, and they have to get an O.K. When they clear one area for us, then Van Ness will have his technicians figuring the exact time and direction for the launching. The whole thing has to be programed very carefully.

It won't take less than two days for the whole thing, if we're lucky. Four days if we're not."

Everyone breathed in slowly. There was a feeling that things were at least moving.

Major Padgett took a hand. "If you are all going to sit here looking gloomy, I've got something to keep you out of mischief. If this thing is going to take place, there's still work to be done on the Dyna-Soar glider. So how about you two fellows coming down to the hangar with me and getting at it?"

"Good idea," said Drummond. "It'll have to be checked out once again, and I think you should all take some thought about fitting it out with extra solid-fuel rockets for maneuvers in space. Once we find out where the Titan is going to be fired from, we'll have to get a transporter plane here, load the glider aboard, and take it over to whatever base that will be. So you fellows have plenty to do."

"We're off," said Mike as the two stood up. "At least it will be better than waiting."

They hurried out, leaving Drummond seated alone, waiting for the call to start his own checking out for the location and time of the desperate launching.

Up in the sky, Stacey's capsule would soon be passing once more over the United States. Joe was feeling worse than he let on. He had made an effort to keep his voice bright and cheerful, and in fact he had suffered from an excess of oxygen, just as had been suspected. Something was wrong with his air valves and he suspected that his air dials were not quite correctly reporting the state of the air in his suit and in the capsule.

His lack of sleep was telling on him, his eyes felt strained. Further he had been jolted rather harder than he'd expected at the take-off and his head ached. He didn't want to report his true condition back to the Earth because he did not want to cut short the expensive project. He was hoping that a little sleep, a little food would straighten him out.

By that time, also, he noticed a new sensation. He was feeling a little dizzy, and the feeling of falling endlessly down an elevator shaft, which is the feeling of utter weightlessness, was beginning at last to put butterflies in his stomach.

By now Joe was beginning to realize that two days in space meant forty-eight long, empty, and rather frightening hours, each hour made up of sixty weightless unnatural minutes. The sky was black, the stars shone brilliant and cold, the Earth below looked so far away and so strangely misty and lost.

Stacey was starting to be spacesick. It was not pleasant.

CHAPTER FIFTEEN

RUSH JOB

HACK SERVISS and Bill Newbold were surprised by the sudden arrival of the two astronauts at their hangar and even more surprised at the orders they received from Major Padgett. They were not in on the secret work of the Quicksilver astronauts, though they had begun to have suspicions from the fact that both Mike and Johnny seemed familiar with space operations.

Padgett did not try to enlighten them further, except for the obvious fact that the Dyna-Soar glider was going to be readied in a big hurry for an actual manned space flight test. The two engineers, like everyone who worked at the Missile Development Center, knew that what went on there was not to be discussed outside the base. They were entirely familiar with the sign that was posted prominently at the entrance to the testing areas:

WHAT YOU SEE HERE
WHAT YOU DO HERE
WHEN YOU LEAVE HERE
LET IT STAY HERE

So they did not ask any questions when they were told the problems facing them and the urgency of them. If they drew any conclusions, they kept their thoughts to themselves. Still, consider their orders:

Ready the glider for flight, see that all solid-fuel rockets are loaded and ready. Attach additional clusters of solid-fuel rockets in both front and rear and rig streamlined protection for them, as well as wire them into the main control panel. Take out certain parts of the ordinary mechanical testing rig in order to make room for a second passenger. Work in a light emergency seat for such a passenger directly behind the pilot (whose seat will be moved forward as much as possible to allow for it). If necessary, shift other components of the glider to make the space. Increase as much as possible the facilities for air renewal.

For a twenty-four-hour emergency job, it was almost impossible. Neither Bill nor Hack could believe it could be done in that time. All the other mechanics at hand in that experimental hangar were called in on the task. "You'll be lucky if we can do it in two days, let alone one," said Hack, already at work.

"You'll have to manage," said Padgett, who was changing into coveralls himself. "Remember what we always say in the service. 'The difficult we do at once, the impossible takes a little longer.'"

A few chuckles greeted this, but after that there

was very little talking besides what was needed on the job—hasty whispered conferences on where does this go, and how do I get that on, and someone give me a number five wrench, and hold this wire a second, till I get this screwed down. . . .

It was dark outside when the phone rang and someone called in from the outer office that it was for Captain Samson.

Mike climbed down from the scaffolding over the glider, wiped his hands on some cotton waste, and went out to the phone. It was Drummond.

"So far," said the colonel, "we've managed to get good co-operation. We still haven't gotten a final O.K. from the Pentagon for the actual flight, but we do have just about everything else.

"We have a tentative agreement to use one of the Titan missile launchers at a SAC base. There were two bases near enough to us for practical work, one in Colorado and one in Arizona. We're going to use the latter as it's closer and more in line with our existing orbital statistics from here. The place is Davis-Monthan Air Force Base, near Tucson.

"We have set a tentative launching time for sixty hours from now. This means that the space glider must be ready for transporting from Holloman in forty-six hours, and we will have a transporter plane ready at the field then. We are allowing time to get the glider to Tucson, to fix it in position in place of the warhead of the missile, and to recheck briefly the setup.

"Holderlin has already got the NASA boys calculating the exact time and programing of the take-off so as to intercept as nearly as possible a transit of Quicksilver Three. We should have that data in another twenty hours. How is your work progressing?"

Mike told him what was going on. "It looks as if we'll be finishing the job on time. A great deal of the groundwork has been accomplished, and the final wiring is what will take the most time tomorrow. But, sir, there is one thing we've overlooked. I will need some means of moving about in space outside the glider. What about that?"

"You're right, Mike, we mustn't forget that. Some simple thing like the failure to include a long coil of strong rope could easily botch up the whole affair. I'll get on it at once. But I have orders for you and Bluehawk now. If you are to make this flight, you must be in top-notch condition. So I am now officially ordering both of you to dinner and immediately after that to bed."

Mike hesitated, for he wanted to finish the task he had been engaged in. But one of his cardinal rules of life, one that he had established for himself when he was just a boy in junior high, was to keep himself physically in good shape. His body was the tool with which his mind and his hopes would achieve the sky. Nobody who used a tool seriously would allow it to get rusted or dulled.

So, it was just a "Yes, sir," with which he signed

off the conversation. Someone else would have to finish the task.

Returning to the glider, he reported the colonel's orders to Johnny and the major. Padgett agreed that the orders were right. Fortunately, at that time, another mechanic had been brought into the plant on a special night shift request, and this man took over the work, as others would later on in the evening, for even the best of men must call it quits sometime.

Mike, Johnny, and the major ate dinner in silence and then drove back to Alamagordo. The major's wife, accustomed to sudden emergency tasks and true to the tradition of an Air Force woman, did not ask any questions. The two astronauts hit the sack in ten minutes, and in one minute more were sound asleep.

Up in the sky, circling the Earth every ninety minutes, Joe Stacey had fallen asleep. For a time he had been quite ill, head dizzy, stomach jumping, and the terrible sensation of seasickness throbbing through him. At Holderlin's orders, he had managed to gulp down some of the pills he was trying out, and very shortly after that his eyes closed and he floated gently in the straps of his seat, asleep.

At the chain of telemetry stations around the world, men sat in silent concentration, watching the beat of Joe's heart, noting the intake and outgo of his breath. Every shift in the temperature and humidity of the capsule was noted, and occasionally a step was taken by remote control to correct it.

Holderlin and Van Ness, neither of whom had taken the kind of advice Drummond gave to Mike Mars, still kept the vigil at Canaveral—their eyes red-rimmed, dozing off in their seats every now and then, drinking black coffee to keep them awake a moment longer, and watching.

"From his respiration, I'd say he was over his nausea," remarked Holderlin at one of the moments when the capsule was passing Florida.

Van Ness nodded. "Hope so," he said. "Sleep and the pills should do the trick."

They were quiet again, and the capsule passed from the trackers in silence.

Sometime in the night the phone rang. Van Ness spoke briefly to someone in Washington, wearily he hung up. "No word yet from the top command. Can't seem to get through to someone who'll risk giving the final O.K., but everything else is apparently all right."

He sat down, put his feet up on another chair, and in a second was asleep again. Holderlin looked at him, then coiled up and tried to nap, himself.

Mike and Johnny and the major were at the hangar early the next morning, refreshed and ready to go. They took over from three mechanics who had worked the night through, and continued the delicate task of rewiring the space glider.

Colonel Drummond showed up a couple of hours later with a bulky package. "Mike," he said, "come down a minute. I want to show you something."

Mike joined him. The colonel unpacked the big box, and Mike looked at the device within. "Why," said Mike startled, "I've seen pictures of that. Is that what you're going to fit me out with?"

"If we can," said the colonel. "You'll stow it in the second seat when you take off, use it when you're up there if you need it. It's Bell's rocket pack for a single man. The one they devised for use by infantrymen for jumping rivers and obstacles. It's a small solid-fuel rocket, fitted as a back pack, and operated from the belt.

"It's kind of clumsy for a space outfit, but it's here and at hand. You should be able to propel yourself in free space with this on."

"Gosh," said Mike. "I used to read Buck Rogers in the comic strips, but I never figured on using one of his flying belts."

"Huh," said Colonel Drummond, "Buck Rogers is just fiction, but this Bell rocket pack is U. S. Army regulation fact."

CHAPTER SIXTEEN

TITAN BASE

It was dark over Davis-Monthan Air Force Base. The sun had set a couple hours before, though the heat of the Arizona desert still lingered about the field. On the vast sprawling base, most of the men were at leisure, their day's work done, eating, or thinking of going into Tucson for the evening, or relaxing quietly with their families. But still there was activity at that base.

One runway in front of the operations building was still floodlighted, and in the ops tower a voice was directing the landing of a large cargo plane that had signaled its readiness to descend. There were other planes on the field—the huge bombers of the Strategic Air Command, some of which were always on the alert—and the crews of these idled in their hangars awaiting the call to duty, should it come.

A few of these men went to the open doors and looked up into the night as the strange plane began its descent. Big planes were an old sight to them and possibly they thought nothing of it, seeing by the light of the field that it was a big heavy cargo plane, a carrier of a type they often saw.

They did not know that it carried a strange cargo, one never before seen on this base, one that could make Air Force history were the secret of its trip ever to be released.

Standing just outside the operations building, Colonel Wyatt of Davis-Monthan stood watching, deep in thought. He was curious, interested, a good deal concerned. He had talked over the phone with his headquarters in faraway Washington and he knew that the question of this strange new mission was still unresolved. However, he would permit the intruders to go through the motions. Whether or not they would ever launch, that was a question that only the next few hours would decide.

The big cargo plane rolled to a halt, swung around, jockeyed into a convenient position signaled to it by the orange-coveralled field men. Its passenger door opened, and a little group of men climbed down.

Mike Mars, one of them, looked around at the dark field, hangar doors open and lit with the eerie presence of giant bombers. "Whew," he said to his companion, the dark-haired young Indian, Johnny Bluehawk. "We're here—and I hope the glider wasn't joggled."

Johnny Bluehawk looked around. "They packed it in carefully, and Hack and Bill are in the cargo hatch with it. Here they come now."

The cargo portal opened and two men jumped

down. "Everything shipshape," called one. "Where's the crew?"

"Here they come now," said Colonel Drummond, dropping to the ground from the front compartment. A couple of trucks were driving up to the cargo plane, along with a jeep. The colonel stepped forward to meet the latter, which carried the colonel of the local base.

There was a hurried low-voiced conversation between the two officers. At a word, the crew of SAC missilemen from the trucks went around to the cargo hatch and under the direction of Hack and Bill began coolly and capably unloading the strange configuration of the Dyna-Soar glider.

Conversation was kept down. These men had worked on many unusual and strange aerospace vehicles, and they knew that time was always the important element in any SAC operation.

The glider was gently lowered from the plane, raised and attached to a low trailer. The men dogged it down, then waited for instructions.

Two days had passed since the hurry-up operation began at Holloman. Two days of swift but careful work on the glider, two days of reading reports on the young man who rode the capsule now circling the Earth once every ninety minutes in a man-made moon that might never return to Earth successfully.

For Mike and Johnny they had been breathless days, days of concealed worry and controlled nerves. Few who had seen the two had realized the emergency under which they had operated. And for Serviss and Newbold it had been a miracle of effort—the glider had been almost torn apart and rebuilt for the new duty that awaited it.

For the astronaut up there, it had been mostly sleep, the monotony of observation, and a certain slight growing anxiety.

For Holderlin and Van Ness, it was a nerve-racking time. They had to conceal their worries from Stacey, and yet they had to persuade the authorities in Washington that only the most daring of risks could save him. Whether that risk was worth the taking was a question left to men who did not personally know any of the people concerned, who had only to consider the expenses of the glider, of the missile, the added risk of the trained astronaut who would make this untested flight. For them the question was: What if they lost the second astronaut too? What if they destroyed the glider as well?

This was the problem that no one in Washington seemed to want to take responsibility for. It had become a sort of game of tag. One officer would pass the decision on to another, and back and forth. First, it was a civilian problem, but the NASA men passed it right back to the Air Force. It would be their man, their Titan missile, and their glider.

The Air Force, reluctant to risk the decision, put it up to higher men in the Defense Department, and these men had first to have the situation explained.

Two days had gone by, and now the hours were ticking away for Joe Stacey and for Mike Mars.

The glider had been loaded, it was now at Davis-Monthan. By daybreak, it was launch—or quit.

Joe Stacey had been told nothing of this. He had been allowed to believe that the command to bring the capsule down out of orbit would be directed entirely from Canaveral. His health had not entirely improved. The oxygen intake in the capsule was still erratic, sometimes apparently all right, sometimes unexpectedly over or under the correct amount. At times he felt sleepier than he should, at other times overexcited.

None of this had contributed to his condition. His head still ached and he felt a tendency to sleep more than was asked of him. Though he had refused to admit his troubles, Dr. Holderlin had determined what was going on for himself. The telemetry didn't lie, and by now the directors of the project were aware that not only had they a maimed capsule to deal with, but an astronaut who was not in perfect condition.

Joe knew that more than forty-eight hours had passed in space, and yet nothing had been said about returning him to Earth. He had watched the line of sunlight and darkness cross the continents of the Earth below more than twice.

He didn't want to ask to be brought down. To call quits, he felt, might reflect on his future ability. He wasn't going to. He'd hold out.

But it was cramped in the tiny space of the satellite. It was hot and sticky from the constant pressure of the high-altitude suit. He was sore from just sitting and waiting. And though the Earth was a constant wonder of changing colors and lands, and the sky was a miracle of black with stars shining and planets visible as never seen from the surface of Earth, they seemed cold to him, reflecting only the vastness of the ocean of space that surrounds our world.

The moon would pass by and he could see its gauntness with the naked eye—the dark oceans that were dry and dusty barrens, the jagged peaks of its airless mountains. The moon was a great sight, but it was not one to warm the heart. Rather it was like the ghost of a world, a dead body shining white and gray and fearful.

From various telemetry stations, Joe heard the voices of Jack Lannigan, Hart Williams and Orin McMahan, and they sounded cheerful. But nobody said anything about coming down.

And Joe heard not a word from Mike and Johnny—that puzzled him, too.

Under the clear Arizona sky the trucks and jeeps rolled across the field, rolled out over the roads, and under starlight moved across the flat desert areas that made up much of the outlying regions of this base. From a seat in one of the jeeps, Mike looked up at the stars and he fancied he could see the capsule pass by—though he knew it would not be visible to the naked eye. He thought of that space, and he wondered briefly what the dawn would hold for him.

Lowering his eyes, he looked across the starlit fields. "It's strange," he said, "there are said to be eighteen Titan launching racks here, and yet I see no gantries, no towers breaking the scene as in Canaveral."

"You'll see," said Johnny. "These Titans are underground until they go into action. It's going to be unusual for us."

They came to a halt. Mike and Johnny got down, looked around. There still seemed to be only the desert. They noticed several large flat cement areas, some gleam of a metal sheath, but nothing outstanding.

As they watched, the glider was unloaded. The colonel of the base came around with Drummond. Then there was motion and change. There was a rumbling, grinding sound, and where there had been flat concrete the ground was sliding open. Floodlights snapped on somewhere, and they saw the opening of a deep pit.

It was the mouth of the silo beneath which was a Titan missile, a giant Intercontinental Ballistic Missile, one of the keys of American defense in the event of global war.

The two young men had barely a glimpse of the floodlighted hole in the ground, the huge wide deep well within which they could just make out the

gleaming sides of a great monster rocket, when Drummond tapped them on the arm.

"Come along," he said. "We go this way. While the SAC missilemen detach the warhead and put the glider into place, you'll be briefed on this setup here."

They followed him and the SAC colonel across the field to a small cement shack. This turned out to be just the entrance to a short flight of stairs down under the ground. The stairs in turn led to a room with a large elevator which they entered. The colonel punched a button, the doors closed, and they descended slowly into the depths beneath the Arizona desert.

CHAPTER SEVENTEEN

SITUATION NEGATIVE

"THESE missile installations are all underground in order to be safe against surprise attack, even of an atomic nature," said Colonel Wyatt as the elevator continued its descent. "After such an attack, they will still be able to operate. If you were here in daytime, you would see very little to indicate that below these level fields are eighteen complex launching racks, blockhouses, and storage areas."

Mike, Johnny, and Colonel Drummond were silent as the elevator came to a stop. It was hard for Mike to determine just how deep they had gone, possibly as much as two hundred feet. "Above us is first the ground, then a thick protective layer of concrete and steel," said the colonel as he led them out of the elevator.

They were in the corridor of a concrete building which in most ways resembled any average working structure of an Air Force installation. Save for the absence of windows, you would not have known you were underground. An air-conditioning system kept a steady soft stream of cool fresh air moving through the corridor, and there was the quiet hum of machines, the faint buzz of men at work, the occasional sound of a footstep somewhere.

"There are several floors here," said the colonel, "all compact and exactly as if this were a building on the surface. We are entirely self-contained, and could hold out here long enough to fulfill all the duties of defense that are required of us."

He led the three along the corridor, down one flight of stairs, and into a small office which was marked as that of the commanding officer. They sat down, ready for the briefing which would precede their efforts of a few hours to come. The colonel looked at them quizzically. "I understand you two captains have done a good deal of study already on missiles. Do you know much about the Titan?"

"Sure, sir," said Mike. "I haven't actually worked with them, but I've seen them at the Atlantic Missile Range and I've studied their construction. For instance, I know that they are probably our leading operative Intercontinental Ballistic Missile, that they are capable of reaching as much as seven thousand miles on the surface to a target or of achieving sufficient velocity to launch a satellite into orbit. The Titan missile is a two-stage liquid-fuel rocket, so perfected as to be capable of being fueled, programed, and launched in an extremely short time after the command is given."

"That's why the Titans have been placed under SAC," put in Johnny Bluehawk. "After their successful flight testing in 1959 and 1960, they have been installed at many bases similar to this one. One thing I never did quite understand is how they can be launched from underground. Sort of like a hole in the ground. It seems to me that launching from a gantry on the surface is far easier to check and correct."

"That was right," said the colonel, "but the problem has been met. There are two types of Titans in operation today. The first is the Titan I, which is actually launched from above ground. Then there is the improved and more powerful model, the Titan II, which can be launched entirely from below the surface.

"Which brings up the point I am going to make for you. This installation, from which you are going to operate—if your plan is O.K.'d—is one of several on our base still using the Titan I. The missile you will use for the glider launching will rise to the surface on its silo elevator before firing."

Colonel Drummond nodded his head, turned to the two boys. "I thought it wiser in this instance to do it that way. An entirely underground take-off might be psychologically disturbing where a manned missile is involved."

Colonel Wyatt rose. "Come along. I'll take you to the central control facility here." They followed him out, down the hall and into a large semicircular chamber. At once Johnny and Mike exchanged knowing glances. "Just like a blockhouse," Mike whispered to his Cheyenne friend.

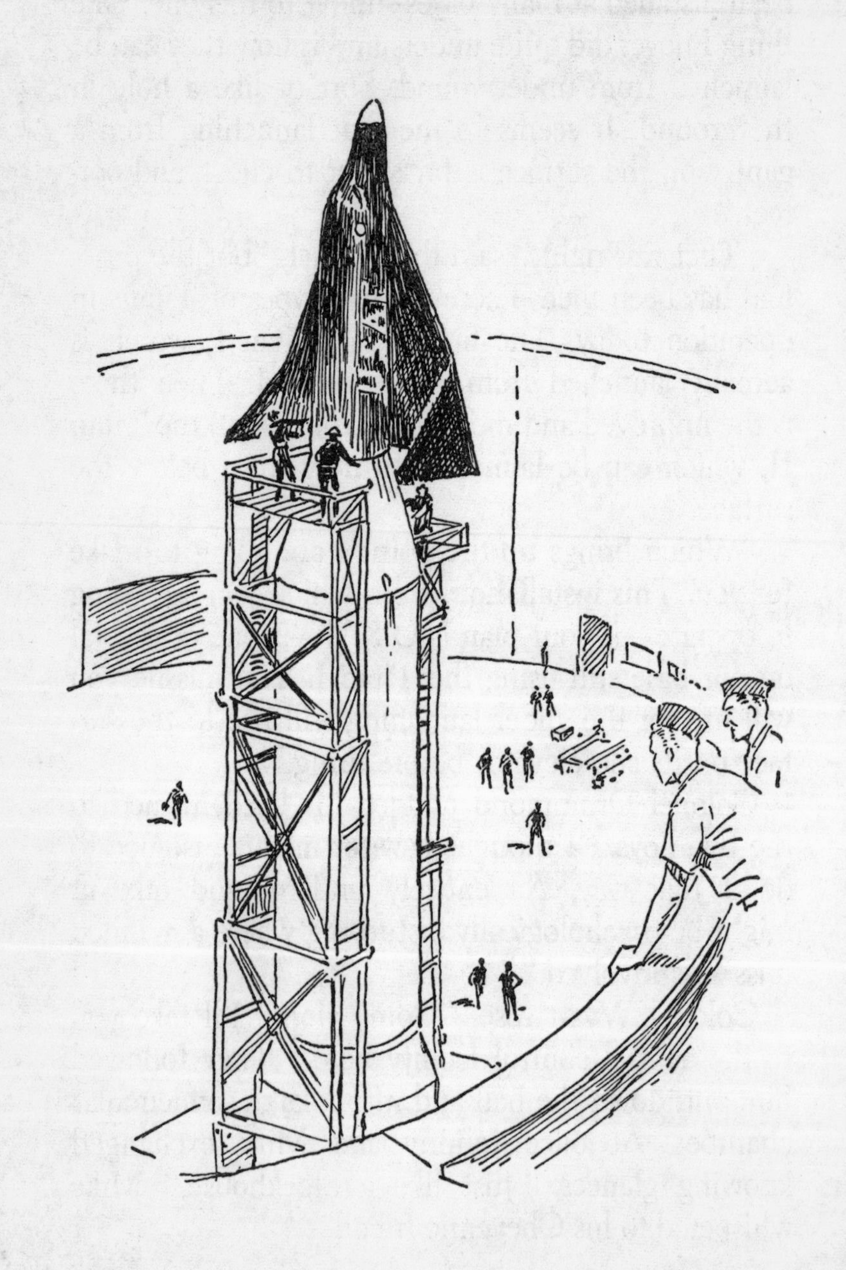

"It *is* a blockhouse," said the SAC colonel, who had overheard. "Exactly the same, performs the same functions."

They stood at the back and looked around. There were the same banks of consoles, with half a dozen men seated before them, checking the readings. There were radar dials, and a wall full of instruments giving the necessary data. Unlike Canaveral, where the blockhouse men were civilians, these operators were all Air Force personnel. This was a military installation, never intended for use by NASA or its projects.

After looking around, the colonel led them out, around a hallway, and toward a thick metal door. This was opened for him by a guard and they stepped through, going through several feet of thickness of wall and down into a narrow tubular passage. "It's several hundred feet to the silo itself," said the colonel. "We still have time to give you a look at it."

They walked the long echoing tunnel in silence. At the far end, a door slid aside and they stepped into a tiny inset balcony. The four stood in silence as they looked about them.

They were in a huge area, like the interior of a gigantic well. Circular walls of concrete hemmed in the sides of this great well, and looking up, Mike could see, many stories above, the dark of the open sky. Filling the well was a great gleaming missile, the body of the Titan II he would ride by daybreak if the command came. There were metallic girders holding it in place and he could make out the shape of a gantry framework at the far side of the tunnel.

Looking up in the light of the blazing lamps that illuminated the whole underground silo, he saw the black-painted Dyna-Soar glider already sitting on the top of the narrower second stage of the great missile. Several tin-helmeted missilemen in coveralls were perched on metal beams around it, evidently making the connections which would hold it in place as firmly as the nose-cone container it carried only a few hours before.

Looking down, Mike saw that coiling vapors of evaporating fuel were already rising like steam. The Titan was loaded, was constantly being reconditioned as the extremely cold liquid gases were lost.

Colonel Wyatt looked at his watch. "Let's get back to my office," he said. "We've got to get this all clear."

They returned to his office. There a phone call to the NASA headquarters at Canaveral brought them the figures for the take-off. It had taken over two days to determine these figures and still it would be touch and go. The capsule, Quicksilver Three, would pass overhead from west to east, slightly north of Tucson, on one of its orbits at a few minutes after daybreak. Its altitude and speed were exactly determined.

At the right time, the Titan would be launched. It would rise, finally put its glider load into orbit at a speed which should be the same as that of the satellite, at the same altitude, and in the same longitude. Theoretically the idea would be to attempt to hit the capsule, but that would be such a target as could not be worked out on such short notice. Instead the aim was to put the glider close enough so that Mike could direct it to overtake and catch the capsule.

This would require very delicate timing. There could be no hitch or delay in the program. If for any reason this morning flight did not take place, it might well be thirty-six or more hours before another launching could be plotted and attempted.

By that time it might be too late to save Stacey. There was a limitation to the amount of air, water, and food in his capsule.

It would be this first flight or never. Both Johnny and Mike understood this perfectly.

Colonel Wyatt marked down the time. "I think it would be wise for you two young men to go back to the surface, go back to the main field, go to the ops building. You can get a bite to eat there, try to get several hours' sleep, and then Captain Samson can change into the flying outfit he'll need for this trip."

Drummond nodded. "You'll find that a space suit similar to the ones we have used in these flights has been shipped in for you and should be there. Be back here at one hour before take-off time."

"O.K., sir," said Mike, and the two took their departure. On the surface, a jeep was waiting to take them back to Davis-Monthan.

The night went fast. They had sandwiches, glasses of milk, then found cots in the ready room and succeeded in getting several hours' sleep in spite of their tension. With a couple hours to go, they were awakened, and Mike went into the suiting room to be fitted into his high-altitude astronaut's outfit.

Johnny Bluehawk was in the main operations office when one of the men behind the desk answered a phone. He looked up. "Anybody know a Colonel Otis Drummond?" he said.

Johnny turned. "Yes," he said. "Are they trying to reach him?"

The desk man nodded. "Want to take the message?" he asked.

Johnny nodded, took the phone. He had just time to say yes, and give his name, before the voice at the other end cut in.

"Will you advise Colonel Drummond that no final decision has yet been made about this flight he's scheduling. Please have him call Washington every half hour to check. We hope to have word shortly."

Johnny felt himself grow a little chilled. He held the phone silent for a moment. Then he spoke carefully, "I'll inform the colonel of your message. And . . . uh . . . may I ask just off the record if you have any idea of what the word is likely to be?"

There was a pause at the other end, a sort of brief laugh, and then the speaker—probably some sort of adjutant or sergeant messenger—said, "I imagine it's going to be negative. They'll play it safe. But they haven't quite made up their minds yet."

"Thanks," said Johnny, and hung up. He turned from the desk, lost in thought, and walked slowly back to the ready room. When he reached it, the silver-suited figure of Mike came out, holding in the crook of his arm his white-painted helmet with its emblem and the initials M.A.R.S.

Mike gave a quick glance at his friend's sober face, and Johnny hastened to force a smile into his expression. "Come on, Mike," he said, "let's get to that jeep and get back."

But all the way back to the Titan silo area, with the dark sky overhead and the stars shining brilliantly in that hour before the dawn, Johnny was silently thoughtful.

CHAPTER EIGHTEEN

ATOP THE TITAN

In spite of the heat of the past day, at that hour of the night the desert was a chilly place. For that reason Mike was not as uncomfortable as he might have been wearing the tight confining suit not as yet connected with an external conditioning system. The first faint hints of the pre-dawn were disturbing the darkness of the sky as their jeep arrived at the silo site.

There were several jeeps and cars parked around, but other than that no one would have suspected the intense activity beneath the sandy waste of Arizona range. Johnny leaped easily down and then helped Mike climb clumsily down in his suit. A couple of airmen in drab coveralls ran up, took hold of Mike's arms.

"This way," one of them said, and they started walking toward a wide concrete area, like a large skating rink set down in nowhere. As they drew near, the concrete seemed to split in half; then slowly, like two colossal half discs, the edges rose up into the air, and Mike could recognize that this was the cover that closed off the top of the Titan silo.

When he and Johnny had looked at it from below,

hours before, those lids had been opened, doubtless to help set the glider down. Evidently they had been closed once the job was done.

He reached the edge, looked down. He could see the shining sides of the missile deep in the pit, still floodlighted, and up at the top, not far below his feet, was the black dart-winged body of the Dyna-Soar glider. A metal scaffolding and ladder descended from the top of the pit. The two airmen assisted Mike down this ladder.

Johnny followed to offer any help. They were beneath the level of the ground, then farther down, until at last the little party stood on a narrow metal platform facing the space glider. Its thick reinforced cabin canopy was slid back. With Johnny's help, Mike stepped forward, was partly lifted across the cowling and helped into the contoured pilot's seat. As the glider was pointed directly upwards, Mike was actually lying on his back in the seat, his feet and hands resting comfortably, quite as he would be when waiting in the capsule for an Atlas launch.

From a speaker concealed somewhere in the outside scaffolding, a voice announced: "X minus thirty minutes, and counting."

The airmen plugged in Mike's various connections, and Mike himself leaned forward and began checking his own controls. Johnny knew he'd now be in contact with the unseen blockhouse.

The airmen pulled away, slid shut the canopy, and Johnny heard it click into place. Then they all went back up the ladder. At the top, Johnny paused to look down. The scaffolding was being drawn automatically away.

Outside it was getting distinctly lighter. Johnny looked around, shivering a bit in the chilly air. He saw a couple of figures come out from the little shack that concealed the blockhouse elevator. In the faint flash of light that came as the door opened and closed, he was sure he recognized Colonel Drummond. The Cheyenne started walking swiftly over to him.

When he reached the colonel, it was Drummond who asked him first. "Any word from back east?"

Johnny hesitated a split second. For an instant the idea revolved in his mind that he could claim the word was favorable, or he could fail to tell Drummond to keep calling back. But duty was duty, so he informed Drummond of the call. "They want you to keep calling back every half hour," he finished.

The colonel frowned at this message. "If they don't come to any decision, this flight is going to go off on schedule. They'll have to make a definite 'No' to stop it now," he commented slowly.

"Wait for me," he said to the others, and then returned to the underground entrance. In a couple of minutes he emerged again. "Still haven't been able to make up their minds," he said. "I said I'll call back in another half hour." He chuckled. "I will, too. But meanwhile . . ."

The colonel turned to Bill Newbold who was with him, gestured to a jeep. "Come on," he suggested.

"Let's get in and drive back to a safe distance. I want to watch this take-off from above."

The three walked over to a waiting vehicle and, climbing in, drove several hundred feet farther away. They stopped the car, got out, turned toward the site of the missile.

The lids that covered the silo were wide open, standing upright on each side, thick two-hundred-ton slabs of steel and concrete. Light was streaming out from the well top they had covered. Now they could see the outline of the glider rising slowly, dart-shaped, sharp-nosed, lighted by the glow from below.

The glider was held upright by a slender rod projecting from a spidery metal tower that was rising along with the missile. As they watched, the body of the Titan began to appear.

Slowly the whole giant missile rose into view, carried up by a powerful elevator upon which the entire structure rested. Gantry and missile and glider rose steadily, eerily reflecting light from the pit, then shining in the pale violet-red of the rising sun.

Even as the Titan rose to the surface, the sun was sending its first rays across the cloudless sky and day was coming with the speed and violent tintings of red that were characteristic of the desert.

By the time the Titan and its holder stood steady at the surface of the desert, the sun was a brilliant blinding orb half over the horizon and the sky was beginning to shade into brilliance. The last star had vanished. The sides of the metal missile reflected brightly in the sun's rays, the red beams tinting the white painted sides ominously. Coils of vapor were rising around the base and for a moment Johnny fancied the thing was a tower, built by some wicked magician on a cloud. He saw the black glider, dwarfed and high up atop this shining eerie tower. And he held his breath.

Bill Newbold was counting to himself, guessing the time left. There wasn't much.

Drummond glanced at his watch. "I imagine that Quicksilver Three must be just coming over the horizon, though we can't see it. Seconds to go."

The Titan was a giant. It stood over ninety-five feet long. Its wide first stage, wreathed in clouds of oxygen and now fast crusting over with frost from the cold element in its liquid oxygen tank, took up about two thirds of the length. The second stage was a little narrower, eight feet in diameter to the first stage's ten, and also now frosting over where its lox tank rested.

Newbold was counting to himself, and Johnny heard him muttering, "Five, four, three, two, one, time . . ."

They watched in silence. Bill's guess was close. The arms of the scaffolding had already slid back. Now there was a faint rumbling, a terrific burst of smoke from the bottom of the missile, a roaring of orange fire blinding to the eyes.

The magician's tower trembled, then began slowly, surprisingly slowly, to rise above the cloud island.

Its speed increased but with maddening precision. Then it seemed to gather strength, to push itself up further, and moved faster away from the clouds which wreathed its base. In a matter of seconds it was up, up above them, rising in full flight, seemingly standing upon a tail of blazing fire. All around the desert the burning tints flickered momentarily.

Then, with a rising ear-splitting roar, it was in the air, going faster and faster. The tiny black glider perched on the top could be seen only as a dot lost in the pencil of white atop the pillar of fire.

The rumbling echoed throughout the area, roared for miles, and the Titan rose, dwindled, its flame flickering to a tiny yellow star in the sky. They watched as it moved over, began to travel toward the east, and finally they lost sight of it in the brilliance of the morning sky.

CHAPTER NINETEEN

RENDEZVOUS IN ORBIT

FROM the moment that Mike had plugged his suit into the board of the Dyna-Soar glider he had been in complete contact with Merlin Van Ness at Cape Canaveral. A relay system had been established whereby the NASA command headquarters at the Cape would hear and speak to him as easily as if he were launching from one of their bases. So Mike could not only hear the local countdown proceeding, but could also take messages from the chief of Space Task Group Q and give them in return.

As he rested comfortably in the seat of the glider, with the countdown coming down to a matter of minutes and the whole setup rising into the air, he had been able to hear a brief rundown from Van Ness as to the position and condition of the capsule he would hunt.

Stacey had gone to sleep several hours before, having been urged to take another dose of the antispace-sickness drugs, though he seemed no longer to need them. "The idea is to keep him sluggish during this attempt," said Van Ness, his voice sounding hoarse and tired to Mike's ears.

"We think it will make your work easier," came the voice of Dr. Holderlin, not sounding much more energetic.

"X minus one minute and continuing," said the voice of the operator in the underground blockhouse. Mike tensed, glanced out the narrow reinforced window.

He could see the sky, could feel the missile he rode rising. There was a brief jolt as it stopped its rise, settled into position. Somewhere he heard a click as the gantry disconnected.

He rested his hands lightly on the seat of his chair. He was cramped up against the board more closely than he had been on the trial flight at Holloman. He quickly let his eyes run over his control board—air, heat, all functioning, all normal. All airtight.

"Twenty seconds," said the voice. The sky was bright and he could see the blue above him lightening as he watched. He wondered for a moment where Johnny was, whether he was watching too.

He braced himself as the count came down. "Easy does it, Mike," whispered the voice of Dr. Van Ness.

"No sweat," remarked Mike quickly, watching the seconds vanish.

Then there was the faint vibration that indicated the touching off of the Titan's first stage. Mike was cool now, resting, just riding.

He felt the pressure build up in his seat as the glider began to rise, pushed on by the huge missile beneath him. The pressure grew and grew, and he watched the G-meter on his board.

The Titan was up now, he estimated, up and going. All automatic, he had nothing to do but sit through it, keep alert for an accident. He could probably jet the glider off if something went wrong, but he felt that it wouldn't. Not with trained SAC missilemen and a tested missile, it wouldn't.

It was to be just himself against the pressure of many gravities. He felt himself being forced back into his seat, and the pressure began to grow with great intensity. He watched through paining eyes as the seconds clicked away on his board. One hundred seconds to go, he thought, that's all. Fifty seconds now, and he was straining, five, six times his own weight and growing. It was like being crushed under a mountain of stone, being ground atom by atom in a great smasher. Eight Gs now and he fought to keep conscious, *must*, *must*, he thought. And it was ninety seconds, ninety-two seconds, ninety-five seconds. . . .

The speed of the rocket was increasing. At one hundred seconds the first stage burned out. The Titan and its glider cargo were going 5300 miles per hour. For Mike there was a split second of release, a moment in which he caught his breath, as if the crusher had slipped, then smack the pressure began again.

The second stage had cut in as the first stage dropped off. Again the pressure mounted, but not

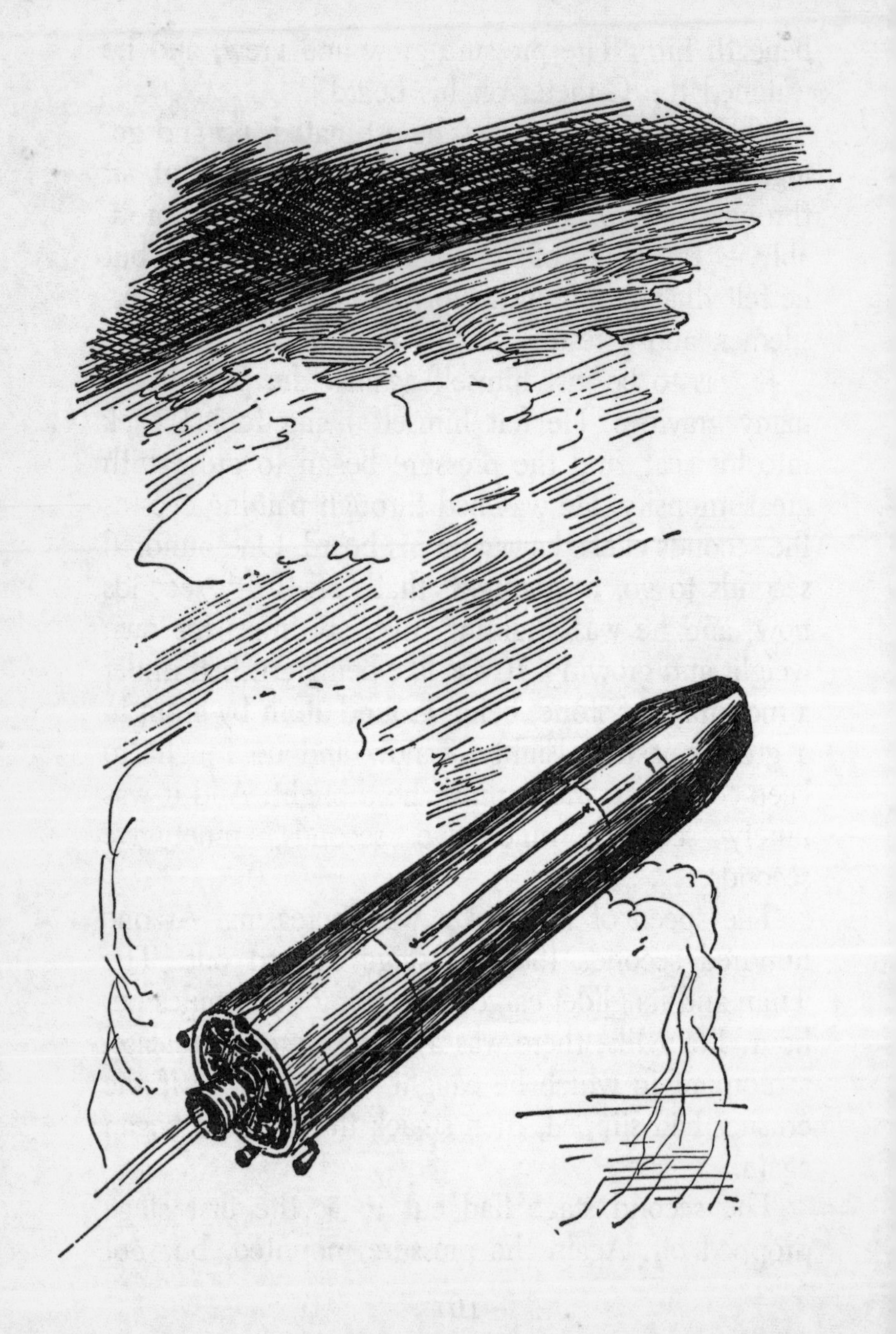

USAF

quite as badly as before; now it was more bearable. The rocket began to tilt as its automatic controls turned it toward the east, turned it so that it would not rise above the orbit that had been set for it. Mike strained once more against the pressure, but this time he was grinning to himself. He had made the worst of it. He'd not blank out on the second stage.

The second stage burned out its main tanks. But the thrust was not over. The smaller vernier rockets were in play, turning the vehicle into the corrected path its cargo would assume. At this point Mike knew that the little vernier rockets would be adjusting all the slight differences that had come up between the plotted path and the actual one the Titan had followed. He steadied his hands on the controls of the glider.

Outside the bright morning sky had vanished. As he had risen, night had returned and as the air had grown thinner, as he passed higher and higher, the blue had changed to black and the stars had returned.

Now he was in the dark of outer space. To all intents and purposes there was no longer atmosphere around his ship and its diminished rocket. The sharp unshielded white lights of the stars glowed untwinkling through his narrow slitted window. Mike was up again, in space.

There was another jolt. Behind him Mike knew the last empty stage of the Titan had disconnected, must have fallen away speedily into the darkness of the sky, to fall through space on its own orbit, leaving a steadily growing distance behind, and finally circling slowly nearer the Earth to burn up as it began to contact the thicker layers of the atmosphere.

He was in control of the glider now, on his own, in orbit at a speed and an altitude that should match that of the capsule from Canaveral.

"In orbit," he spoke into his helmet phone. "Everything checking O.K."

"You should be almost directly in the track of Q-3," said Van Ness. "Watch for it."

Mike squinted his eyes. He was floating free now, weightless, but with his suit fastened to the seat the sensation was one of lightheadedness—not of any great discomfort. He had been through this before; his body, as if remembering the previous experiences, rapidly began to adjust. There was a brief instant of the sensation of falling, but he swiftly shut his mind to that and regained control.

Somewhere ahead should be the capsule. He couldn't see it, mightn't see it until he was fairly close. But he was aware that down below, on the surface of the Earth, his position and that of his target were accurately traced in the telemetry stations of NASA.

"You are about six miles behind and a half mile above," came Van Ness' voice. "Here are your coordinates and the capsule's." He read off the figures. Mike ran his hands across the controls, pushed a stud. One of his tiny rockets flared briefly somewhere on the upper area. There was a faint pressure on his body as the glider dipped down, began to respond to the rocket by coming closer in its orbit. From Canaveral the voice of Van Ness directed him. "You're nearing level, you're on level, hold it." With a flick, Mike steadied the glider again.

"Now, creep up on the capsule. You should be able to see it visually," Van Ness said.

Mike flicked on another rocket, one set in the tail of the glider. Slowly the glider increased its speed, though there was no visual evidence of that to be noticed through the observation window. There were the stars, and their distances were so great that no change in speed could make a difference. Mike leaned forward, caught a glimpse of the rim of the Earth, just a faint hint at the bottom of his visibility. It appeared as a hazy edge.

He strained his eyes. There was a star; that couldn't be the capsule. There, what was that flicker of light in the darkness? No, it must be a far-off star. Again, was that something? Didn't seem like it.

He watched intensely as his glider moved silently in its temporary orbit. Somewhere below him, he guessed, he must be passing over the southern United States; Texas may have been already left behind. Left to itself the glider would circle the Earth in an hour and a half. He'd be over Florida by the time he spotted Stacey—if he did.

He strained his eyes, remained tensely silent for a time. He could even hear the faint intake of Van Ness' breath on his earphones, but nothing was said.

There was an odd flicker in the sky. Against the blackness, against the stars, something faintly reddish moved, like a spark. He focused on it, watching. Yes, it was moving also, passing the stars, crossing them. It seemed to flicker a bit, like a tiny red spark in darkness.

Was that the capsule? If it were painted red, it was. Was Q-3 painted red? He whispered the question to the ground. Back came the answer, "Yes, it's red-orange in color."

"Then I have the object in sight, sir," said Mike softly. He heard a faint sigh as if of relief in his phones.

Slowly the glider drew closer to the glinting red spark and as slowly the source of the flickering light became clearer and clearer.

It was a Mercury-type capsule. It was like a boy's top floating alone in space. Mike could see the sun glinting from its scarlet painted sides. He saw the tiny dark circle that was its one window. He could make out the lettering on its side: UNITED STATES and NASA Q-3. Mike waited until he was as close to it as he would come. His glider was not exactly on its level. It was still perhaps a couple hundred feet farther out than the capsule and moving slightly faster.

Now he began some delicate jockeying. A touch on a rocket here, a touch there, in and out, sometimes seeming to fall unexpectedly away from it, sometimes rushing past it.

At last he stopped. "I think I'm as close as I can make it," he said to Van Ness. "About a hundred feet away, about two o'clock from Q-3."

"O.K., Mike," said Van Ness' voice. "Think you can cross the distance?"

"I'll try, sir," said Mike. "What's the condition of the capsule's passenger?"

"Still asleep," said Van Ness. "Want him awake or remaining comatose?"

"Might be better to leave him inactive, sir," said Mike, remembering the risks of panic such as occur during swimming rescues. There might be elements of that here.

"As you think best," said Van Ness. "When are you going to make the jump?"

"Right now, sir," said Mike. "Disconnecting from the board, with your permission."

"Go to it," said Van Ness, his voice suddenly fading with strain.

Mike unplugged the radiophone connection, began to prepare to leave the glider.

CHAPTER TWENTY

A ROPE ACROSS SPACE

MIKE closed his helmet, sealed his suit. Rapidly he unstrapped himself from his seat, disconnected all other connections. Automatically his suit's internal air system shifted to the two air tanks resting by his seat. He lifted them, bending forward, and slung them into position on his back. Should be enough air to keep going for about forty minutes, Mike thought.

He reached out, adjusted a valve on his control board. Immediately a faint hissing sound reached his ears through the helmet. It would be the last sound he'd hear from outside his suit, for it meant that he had set the inside air controls to equalize the pressure with that outside the glider. Since there was virtually no pressure outside the glider, this meant that the air within would be exhausted. When there was no longer air inside the Dyna-Soar, he could open the canopy without the danger of being jarred out by a rush of air.

Mike reached behind him into the spare seat which had been rigged there. Secured on it was the

USAF

Bell rocket belt system, and he hefted this across, squeezing it over the seat to his side.

Fitting it would be a problem, considering the tanks already on his back. He pushed it around and fastened it loosely. When he was outside he'd adjust it correctly. Already the hissing of escaping air was becoming inaudible. He watched the pressure dial dropping, then it reached zero. Mike now picked up the long coil of nylon rope which was stowed near his feet. He carefully tied one end of the cord to the arm of his seat. He carefully unrolled the cord, letting it drop in long untangled loops until he had the other end available. This he knotted about his middle like a belt.

He rose to a crouching position, as high as he could within the confines of the glider. Then he thrust back the canopy.

There was no pop of air. It slid back and he looked

up and out into the vast blackness of empty space. Glancing down again to keep oriented, he stood up, his head coming above the level of the open glider.

Carefully he pushed upward. His weightless body drifted up from the inside, the rope paying out as it did so. And then he was outside the glider, holding on with one hand.

He glanced around. He could see the red metal side of Q-3 glistening in the unshielded sunlight. He reminded himself not to look in the direction of the sun. He couldn't afford to have his eyes temporarily blinded by that intolerably glowing disc. The rocket belt came up now, and Mike worked it around into place, fitting it loosely over his air tanks. It must have bulked very high on his back—it was not intended for space use, but it had been handy and available. NASA hadn't yet mass-produced any of the several experimental space-motion systems that Mike had seen on visits to Wright-Patterson's laboratories.

Mike took a deep breath. He was ready now. He turned in the direction of the capsule. It hung there, seemingly motionless. You would not realize that both it and the black dart-like glider were moving through space at over 18,000 miles an hour. Below, the Earth was a mass of blues and greens and yellowish browns. The shine of sunlit ocean made a glare from most of what was now beneath. They were over the Atlantic now.

During his training period, he had done a lot of underwater swimming, SCUBA diving with mask and air tank. The purpose of those hours of water exercises was now to be realized. Motion in space would resemble underwater motion in many respects.

He turned to the capsule, directed his eyes at it, and then pushed off. Slowly he moved through space, for a moment a celestial body on his own, the nylon cord paying out behind him.

As he floated through space, hanging between heaven and Earth, with nothing between him and stars save the thin skin of his suit, he recited to himself a little poem that he had made up years back while in school. It was a poem he often said in conditions of grave danger and emergency, and he said it now to remind himself of his dream and his hopes:

"Michael Mars is my name,
America's my nation,
Space flying is my game,
And Mars my destination!"

Halfway between the two man-made objects, he saw that he would have to correct his direction. Were he underwater, a wave of his hands, a kick with his back flippers would do it. Here there was nothing to kick against. He reached for the studs of the rocket belt, twisted his body directionally, and pressed.

Instantly he jerked sharply forward as the rocket flared briefly. He seemed to plunge headlong at the capsule, and he managed quickly to twist the rocket and reverse its speed. Just in time he came to a near halt a few feet from the side of the capsule.

Glancing back, he saw the nylon line reaching out, like the thin strand of a spiderweb shining in the sun, between him and the now distant figure of the glider. He couldn't make it out very well, for it was black and between him and the sun.

He turned back and saw that he was within touching distance of the capsule, his momentum not having totally ended. He reached out with a gloved hand, and his fingers scraped against it.

Mike drew himself to it, clung to it. He then crawled gently around the wide lower edge until he came to the indentations that marked the side hatch. He reached into his belt for a small wrench, got it out, reached out to begin unscrewing the hatch cover.

Then he paused as a sudden thought struck him. If Joe Stacey was asleep and his helmet open, opening that hatch could easily cause his death. The air inside would shoot out (he reminded himself to keep his body clear of the opening), and Joe would be suffocated as it did so.

Nothing had been said about this. He recalled then that during Johnny Bluehawk's sleep in orbit, he had been ordered to seal his suit. This was a simple precaution against any accidental puncturing of the capsule while the astronaut slept. So, then, closing the suit while sleeping was presumably to be standard practice.

Mike told himself that surely similar instructions must have been given to Joe during the course of his stay in space. Mentally crossing his fingers (physically he couldn't), Mike began to take off the hatch cover.

It went slowly but he encountered no trouble. First one bolt, then another, then finally the hatch slid out in his hands as he pushed against it. The underhatch was exposed. With a simple shove, this would unseal. Mike clung to the capsule with one hand, punched the cover with the other.

It shot out like a cork from a shaken-up fizz bottle. With it, Mike knew had gone the air inside the capsule. He swung himself quickly across the vent, slid himself halfway inside the capsule.

Joe was there, suit sealed, helmet fastened, eyes closed in sleep. Joe was about a foot from Mike as he looked in. He pushed himself further into the narrow space, reached out, and began to unsnap the suit connections, mentally checking them off as he did so.

For a moment he entertained the idea of briefly plugging his own phone connection into the capsule's board and reporting his progress. But that, he told himself, was wasting valuable time. They'd know, the moment that Joe's connections were severed, that he was there.

He pulled at Joe's body. Stacey floated free from the contour seat, his head rolling, still sound asleep. Backing out, Mike kept a grip on Joe's suit and pulled him along. He twisted about, outside, then began to ease Joe gently through the open hatchway.

As Joe was nearly out, Mike glanced at his face.

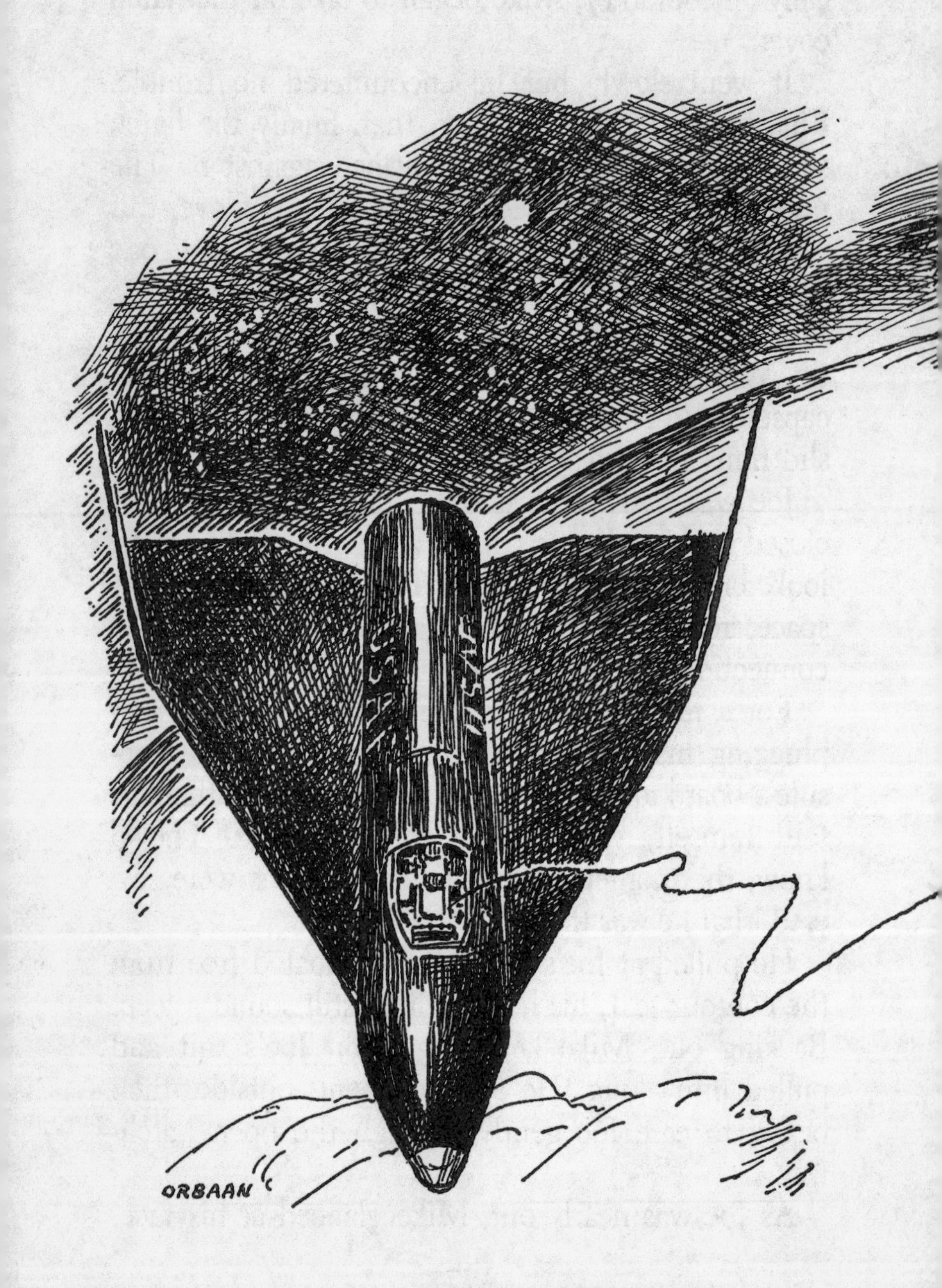
ORBAAN

Joe's eyes flicked open for an instant; he seemed to look sort of sleepily at him, his mouth opened as if he had said something, and then his eyes closed again.

"Joe'll figure this as a bad dream." Mike spoke aloud to himself.

Now Stacey's silvery-suited figure was outside the capsule, limp and motionless. Mike pulled in on the slack of the nylon line, made a loop in it, and slid it over Stacey's head, tightening it about his waist. Then, holding Joe with one hand, he drew in the nylon cord until it was taut. He pulled on it sharply and felt himself start to move in the direction of the glider. Holding Stacey, Mike floated easily and safely back, drawn by the cord, which he pulled in and pushed behind him as he went.

The two came to a bump against the black side of the long dart-like glider. Mike hefted the sleeping astronaut's body—being weightless certainly had advantages, he said to himself—over the open cockpit and, bracing himself, slid him into the second seat. Then Mike climbed over himself, untied the cord from his waist, and tossed it out into space.

The rocket belt came next. Room was now too limited, and without hesitation he tossed that out into the depths of space. "They'll take it out of my salary," he said to himself, "destruction of government property," and smiled.

He slid down into the pilot's seat. Twisting around, he pushed Stacey into a better sitting position and buckled the seat belt around him. Then he resumed his own seat, fastened himself in, replugged into the board.

He reached up, slid the canopy shut, clicked it airtight. Then he punched the board to resume normal atmospheric pressure.

"Mike?" said a voice in his ear. "What's the situation?"

"A-O.K., sir," he said. "Mission accomplished. Can you give me my present co-ordinates?"

"Very good," said a voice he almost did not recognize. It was Van Ness', but suddenly so choked that it was out of pitch. Mike swallowed, realizing the tension that must have been riding the director.

"Holderlin here," said a new voice, that of the space medicine director of Quicksilver. "Here are your co-ordinates. You are nearing Hawaii, and you should consider starting re-entry at your convenience."

Hawaii? Mike started. That had taken a longer time than he'd thought, that simple trip across space to the capsule. He glanced through the window, looked down. Sure enough, the Earth was in darkness. He had passed through the day, had entered the night again.

For a moment he mused on the oddity of it. He had taken off from Arizona just at sunrise. He had ridden through the entire day to come, had crossed over back again into the night that he had left behind and was again about to come back to the zone of the sunrise. It would be actually an hour and a half later, yet for him an entire day, if you wanted to look at it that way.

Mike jotted down the figures he'd been given, glanced over his board.

Pressure normal, temperature normal, everything functioning. This would be a lot like the X-15 over again, he thought.

He rode the orbit until he saw the line of sunrise below him, the line that divided his home planet between night and day. The coast of California was beneath him. He flicked on his retro-rockets.

The space glider began to descend as its speed in orbit was reduced.

CHAPTER TWENTY-ONE

CARGO FROM Q-3

THE temp gauge on Mike's dial began to climb. Mike watched it tensely. The temperature on his glider's nose was going up steadily as the air thickened. He glanced to one side. He couldn't see his wings; at this point they only started, flaring out, but he would bet the tips were getting hot.

He watched the temp gauge like a hawk. Behind him Joe Stacey was still sleeping, though he could faintly hear his breath with now and then a slight mumble as if he were saying something in his sleep.

When the temp began to register dangerously, and he could spot a faint reddening in the visible nose of his ship, Mike worked his rockets. The speed of drop was stopped, he turned the glider, went upward a way, then began to drop again. The temp gauge slid backward as the heat diminished, then once again began to climb as he resumed his drop into the thicker air.

Now began a series of such exercises, a time-consuming affair of downward drops, of rising heat on wings and body, of relief when Mike would pull out of it, then again the downward drop. Each time the

USAF

glider was working itself lower and lower, reaching thicker and thicker layers of air.

Speed was diminishing steadily each time Mike bumped his way down. He had to get the glider under some sort of reasonable control.

Again he swooped downward into the air, the ground now perhaps forty or fifty miles below him. The glider began to light up on the outside, the heat turning its wings red and its nose firing up first to red and then to white hot. Mike pulled up at the last second, but he had achieved a good deal of his objective.

Once again—now, he felt—now I can do it. The glider came in at a gentle angle, but at what was still a fearful speed, a record-breaking speed for an aircraft. He could hear the whistling and straining in the body; there was a vibration. The black dart began to bounce violently as it encountered air resistance. Mike held on, kept it going. The heat was rising too much; he sighed, pulled it out once again.

And finally it was in for good. Tearing, booming its way down, red hot on wings and nose. He'd made that part of it, Mike told himself, and reported the matter to the ground. Someone, he did not recognize the voice, told him his present position.

"I'm in gliding capacity now," Mike said. "Where would you suggest I take her in?"

"If you can swing around in a wide circle, why not take her in at Edwards?" said the voice from the ground. "I understand you know the field, and it has the facilities for a gliding high-speed landing."

"Good idea," said Mike. He looked for his present position. He was somewhere over Kansas, he guessed, about twenty miles up and traveling mighty fast. He began to direct his glide; he brought the black Dyna-Soar dart around in a huge circle, swinging it north, then around, always lower and lower and slower and slower. By the time he was crossing Utah he was ten miles up and doing 2000 miles an hour. Over Nevada he was seven miles up and coming to a more reasonable speed.

By the time he was crossing the Mojave Desert he was under control, flying a fast glider under conditions not too abnormal.

He remembered the approach maneuver for the X-15 as a landing glider. He repeated it, with the tower at Edwards Air Force Base directing him. He came over the series of great dry lakes that ringed that famous testing center for missiles and planes. Then, almost as he had done before, he circled in and brought the glider down in a swooping, drag-parachuted stop on Rogers Dry Lake just outside Edwards.

There was a huge cloud of dust as his skids dragged across the flat hard level of the onetime lake bottom. And then with a shudder, the Dyna-Soar glider came to a halt, its outside burned and blistered but the two people inside safe and sound.

When the ambulance and the cars from the base

got to the glider, they found two sleeping men. Joe Stacey had not awakened, and Mike, who had not had a full night's sleep before his take-off, was slumped in his seat, snoring softly.

That evening there was a sort of quiet party at one of the tables in the Officers' Club at Edwards. Otis Drummond had flown in from Tucson as soon as he had heard the news of the safe landing, and with him had come the technicians Hack Serviss and Bill Newbold, who were as anxious to look over their pet project, the glider, as was the colonel to check out, personally, his two sky-wandering astronauts. And of course Johnny Bluehawk had come along to be in on the news of the trip.

Mike Mars was in good spirits. There was a certain relief in having the dangerous mission over and done with. He had taken another step up the ladder of space, and thereby he felt himself just that much closer to the day in the future when he would set foot on the surface of the red planet, from which he took his nickname.

"So I called back to Washington a half hour later, just when I said I would"—Colonel Drummond continued telling his account of the take-off—"and before they could tell me what they had decided, I told them the shoot had already come off. The big brass I spoke to somehow never got around to saying what they had decided. My guess is it must have been a no—but it was too late."

"And a darned good thing it was," said Bluehawk

"Considering that the medics in the hospital here say that Joe Stacey would have been in really serious shape if he'd stayed in orbit another two days. Apparently the bang he took on his skull when the trouble came at the start would have become infected badly in just a few hours."

"Are we going to tell Joe how he got down to the ground?" asked Mike. "I'm sure he doesn't know yet. The doctors haven't told him."

"Oh, I guess we'll break it to him gently," said the colonel. "He'll make a fast recovery. You astronauts are a tough bunch of youngsters, for all that. It's Doc Van Ness who is going to need a rest from the tension."

Mike and Johnny laughed a bit. Then Hack put in a question and the discussion changed to other things than the fortunes of the Space Task Group Q space fliers. But though those fortunes were unknown to the happy group at that table that evening, they were to have more exciting adventures in space and between the planets. For there were many plans and projects on the drawing boards of NASA, and even that day one had been taken out and was being scrutinized.

Watch for a new adventure in the conquest of space in the next Mike Mars book.